Misfortune's Lady

A Scandal in Surrey novel

Sandra Sookoo

Adventure. Humor. Inclusion. Romance

New Independence Books

Published by New Independence Books and Sandra Sookoo
Ebook ISBN: 9781301771912
Print ISBN: 9798201501297
Contact Information:
sandrasookoo@yahoo.com
newindepdencebooks@gmail.com
Visit me at sandrasookoo.com
Book Cover Design by Sandra Sookoo
Photo: Deposit Photos
Publishing History
First Digital Edition, 2013
Second Digital Edition, 2022
First Print Edition, 2022

Blurb for Misfortune's Lady

She wants a slower pace... Miranda Ellis Mason Craythorne is three times a widow. Some say bad luck has dogged her steps; she rather thinks it's just life, yet the rumors sting. She's long left her wild youth behind and now lives at her country estate, content to play matchmaker. Seeing John sets fire to the *tendre* she's carried for him and causes her to rethink remaining in widowhood even though avoiding matrimony is for his own good.

He wants to settle down... Mr. John Goddard has admired Miranda from afar for years, but their timing has never been right. As a Bow Street Runner-turned-private investigator, he knows mortality has an expiration date. What better woman to start a family with than the one he's held a torch for? But his penchant for the occasional ménage might sour the plans.

He wants the next exciting game... Richard Howick, who is rarely on home soil, is a spy who wants nothing more than the next adventure. He's giving life a merry chase and has no plans to domesticate. He's too much of a rake not to take pleasure when it's offered, and the opportunity to play the occasional third thrills him.

Life presents an unorthodox chance... While rumors abound and scandal nips at their heels, between the three, desire explodes. If their luck holds, they might just find love in the mix.

Dedication

To Rebecca Poole. You're always so excited every time I talk about my Regency stories. I appreciate that as well as the support. Enjoy!

Author's Note

While this story is set at the end of the Regency time period, I'm of the opinion that both men and women in this era had the ability for forward thinking and could have shown this in their actions as well. No one ever moves forward unless the status quo is challenged.

As such, I have taken a bit of literary license with my characters and the world in which they reside in the hopes that it will bring this period to life with a bit of different perspective. The fact these characters are completely naughty and not regretful of their behavior lends another level to the genre. It doesn't mean they're not "real" Regency stories, it merely means they're a different brand of stories.

Also, you won't find any simpering young misses straight out of the schoolroom or starry-eyed debutantes here. Neither will you find high-born dukes or gentlemen dripping with riches. The characters in this series are older and have some "life experience" on them. The stories in my Scandal in Surrey series are also highly erotic in nature. Misfortune's Lady is no exception and it is a m/f/m *ménage*. I hope you enjoy!

Chapter One

September, 1820

Near Yorktown, outside Cambridge Town in Surrey, England

Mrs. Miranda Ellis Mason Craythorne nodded and smiled to acquaintances as she passed through the crush of guests filling her brother's country manor. Candles flickered in air currents disturbed by the milling throng. Floral perfume, talc powder and the scents of crisp soap and candle wax wafted into her nose. A few overly loud feminine titters punctuated the low buzz of conversation flowing around her. Though she loved having people in her home for this special gathering, she searched for two men in particular. She'd invited them to the rout to see if they'd suit her second-cousin, Miss Annabelle Lythe. The young lady had made no secret of her place on the Marriage Mart, and Miranda wanted to try her hand at matchmaking. One of the men she had a fleeting—if vaguely intimate—acquaintance with, while the other she knew of just by name. Surely between them, her cousin could find favor, and if not, well, men were always in abundance.

Except, the two gentlemen in question had either not yet arrived or she'd missed them. She threw another glance around the crowded drawing room but came away disappointed. The last time she'd seen Mr. John Goddard, she'd been in London with her third husband at a glittering function for diplomats and various members of Parliament. Though he'd escorted a woman and she had been recently married, she couldn't deny the swift connection that had grown between them the moment their hands had touched in passing. She'd heard through the gossip mill he remained unattached. Even now, a tiny twinge flitted through her lower belly. He was the epitome of everything a good husband should be—just not for her, but he'd be a great catch for her cousin.

"Wonderful party, Mrs. Craythorne." Lady Ashford, striking in a black gown sparkling with jet beads, stepped into her path. "Brilliant arrangement of tables in the card room. I might just win some pin money."

"I'm glad you're enjoying yourself, Sybil. I shall join you later." She patted the woman's shoulder and continued on while her mind fixated on John—the man who'd always managed to slip away.

Her smile faltered. If there had ever been a gentleman she'd wanted to attract for a potential fourth husband, it would have been him, yet marriage wasn't a natural state for her. She was happy with her life as it was now, and she had no wish to doom another man to an early demise. John had been a dream from another time and that was where he must remain. A man like him would most likely desire heirs, and she'd never been blessed with good fortune in the fertility realm. His goals would align nicely with her cousin's for Annabelle had made no secret of her wish to reproduce.

As Miranda navigated the gathering, she let the excitement in the atmosphere wash over her. Her smile returned as the ennui faded. She might not have had long terms with her own matches, but she could lend her expertise with marriage to others. Before the evening's event closed, she would locate both men—if they were indeed still in attendance—and introduce them to Annabelle. If things went well, it would be her first success as an unofficial matchmaker.

As she spied a young pair making calf's eyes at each other, she sighed in appreciation. Every woman should experience the wonder and joy that came with the beginning of a love match. The thought widened her smile and confirmed her decision to move forward with her decision to help couples navigate the often muddied waters of the Marriage Mart. Pledging lives to each other should go beyond wealth and Society connections. Love and desire should be taken into account as well. If the match was good, it could be very, very good indeed. The heat and passion a woman gained in the marriage bed had the power to set her free and give her the confidence to do anything she wished.

"Miranda, there you are. I've been looking everywhere." The breathless announcement preceded Annabelle as she rushed to Miranda's side. An uplifting tinkle of a pianoforte followed in her wake as the performer struck up a lively tune from one of the side rooms.

"You've found me." She admired her cousin. Tall and willowy thin, the young woman, though past the first blush of youth, still managed to seem ethereal in her blonde beauty. At four and twenty, the younger woman's fondest dream was to marry well and have a dozen babies. Annabelle wanted nothing more than to settle into family life. Finding a like-minded gentleman, to date, had proved difficult. Many men were not driven to set up their nurseries immediately nor did they desire so many children. Tonight, clad in a light blue gown with the low-cut bodice hugging her small chest, there was no doubt in Miranda's mind Annabelle would leave with a few prospects. That was to say she'd find success until the young lady opened her mouth and spouted off her urge to procreate quickly and often. "How may I be of assistance?"

Annabelle's almond-shaped brown eyes sparkled with deviltry. She rapped her folded fan on Miranda's knuckles. "I wanted to thank you for the effort you put out on my behalf."

"It's not all for you, dear girl." She paused near a grouping of potted ferns. "If the evening is successful, I might offer some of the debutantes, and a few select young men, my services as a matchmaker." She waved to a female acquaintance, pleased when the rotund woman glared and quickly turned away. Lady Underhill had never accepted her in Surrey society, but Miranda never passed an opportunity to be sweetly polite to her. "Those who are in desperate need of help, of course."

Annabelle followed her gaze. "Do you plan to start with one of that dragon's sons?"

"Good heavens, no." Miranda drew her cousin close and lowered her voice. "Since Lady Underhill's daughter, Vanessa, caused such a scandal with her own beau a couple of months ago, the good woman has gathered her sons even closer. I don't believe anyone could break through those reinforced leading strings." She didn't mind indulging in an *on dit* or two, especially when the gossip involved a person who favored herself above all others.

The younger woman tittered behind a gloved hand. "Is Vanessa here this evening? I'd like to ask her for pointers. She landed a viscount, after all, without help from anyone, in less than a week if the rumors are to be believed."

"No." Miranda rolled her eyes. "The last I heard she was happily ensconced with her husband near the Lake District." She liked to think she'd played a small role in the woman's current martial state even though it had only been tongue-in-cheek guidance. "As I mingle, though, I fear I lack excitement."

"Oh, pish-posh. I've never known you to worry about that before now."

"I haven't, but that doesn't lessen the sting at times." Which was why she enjoyed her tucked-away lifestyle in the country.

Annabelle cocked her head to one side. "In all honesty, you've grown dull since your last husband died. I mean, you've not even invited any of your guests—or me—to stay the night afterward. We're all forced to travel home in the dark through the country."

"Yes, and that is my prerogative. I value my privacy too much to wish for lingering guests. This is a rout not a house party. You could have turned down the invitation."

"True, but how bland you are, cousin."

A tiny pang of regret tugged at her heart. "Perhaps I am, but I certainly don't feel it. In my mind, I'm as gay and exciting as I was when I was your age. I've just grown a few more curves." In fact, she'd recently had the modiste let out the seams on a few of her most favorite gowns. She adjusted the loop of the black lace fan on her wrist.

Amusement flickered through Annabelle's expression. "All to the good. I'm surprised men aren't trailing after you by the dozens."

"Don't be silly. We both know I'm too old for suitors, so your flattery is useless." Miranda stopped short of snorting her derision. "After tonight, I'll most likely burrow back into my quiet life and be thankful for the solitude." She didn't want the admirers. At the last second, she stopped a sigh. Men underfoot would be an annoyance to be sure, but at times it would be nice to be the center of someone's world again.

"Nonsense, cousin. You're merely on the cusp of turning thirty. That isn't ancient and it's not told enough to bury yourself away."

"Of course it's not, but I do so enjoy home life."

"You're dull. Even your fresh-faced looks won't help that." Annabelle snickered.

Silly woman. What was boring to her was exciting to Miranda. "I cannot help that I enjoy my birds and gardening."

A false pout touched Annabelle's lips. "I couldn't wait to be grown, if only to follow in your brazen footsteps. You seemed to have such fun in your travels and with your men. Your uninspired domestication disappoints me."

A surprised bout of laughter left Miranda's throat. "I do apologize. I suppose my previously wild reputation has soured my reception in many circles still."

"No doubt from jealousy. Yet you've put down roots in Surrey. The local dragons hate you. You know that, right?"

"I had to domesticate at some point. Why not do it in Surrey, especially since my brother offered this property?"

"That isn't the issue. I won't lie and say country air hasn't agreed with you, but you need to be matched instead of trying it on everyone else." Annabelle shook her head. "It's been two years, Miranda. I thought you enjoyed the wedded state?"

She stifled the exasperated sigh building inside. This was but one of the reasons she'd rather spend her time out of the public eye. Why did everyone assume she needed to wed again in order to be happy? "I *did* enjoy being married; however, luck hasn't been on my side as evidenced in the unfortunate demise of all three husbands." She twirled an escaped curl at her temple around a forefinger. Blonde that held reddish highlights under the right circumstances—it had always been a source of pride.

"Oh, that's why the gossips call you Misfortune's Lady." Enlightenment filled Annabelle's expression and her Cupid's bow mouth curved into a sly grin. "I always wondered. Mama would never tell me the full story."

Faint warmth crept into Miranda's cheeks. *Blasted rumormongers.* "Yes, even though life in the public eye and I have parted ways, I never lived down that lovely little moniker."

"Perhaps you should reacquaint yourself with scandal then. Come up to London with me and take in the Little Season. We have enough time before it starts to have gowns made and shop for hats and everything else. It'll help you forget about life's disappointments."

"That's very nice, but I do not consider my marriages disappointments. I learned much from each husband." Was that what everyone thought, that she'd accomplished nothing and was a failure since all of her husbands were dead?

"It's been an age since you saw Mama and Papa." Excitement lit Annabelle's eyes as she warmed to her topic. "Do say you'll come!"

Good heavens, a trip to London is not what I want.

That would mean she'd need to leave her beloved home in order to mingle among the very crowd she used to cavort with years ago. They were too fast for her now, too much absorbed in shallow pursuits. Yet, she owed Annabelle an answer. "I shall think about it." She touched her cousin's arm when a real pout threatened. "Don't fly into the boughs. London simply isn't on my agenda at the moment." Though a mere six years separated her from Annabelle, life experiences had vastly expanded the gap.

Annabelle tossed her head. "I'd wager you'd change your mind if a man were involved."

"Perhaps, but then, I am not searching for a match." The crush of people around them grew as partygoers entered the drawing room from the open terrace doors. "If you will excuse me a moment, I must see to the other guests. I believe it is beginning to rain."

An unladylike giggle followed the rejoinder. "So much social stimulation might tempt you into something you might not like."

Miranda ignored the jab. No longer did she want to openly court gossip. Those days were well behind her. "We'll talk again soon, perhaps over whist later?" When her cousin nodded, Miranda slipped into the crowd. At times, having the focus on her was cloying, which was ironic since she'd spent a good portion of her married life creating scandal after scandal. Stealing the Duke of Rouden's prized stallion and relocating the animal into Hyde Park was only one such incident. In a way, being leg-shackled thrice had tamed her.

She stood in one of the open doorframes. Those urges had never gone away. She'd merely directed the energy into other things. That was her little secret. In the two years since her last husband had died, there had been no one to coax her attention from domestic chores—

Her gaze landed on a tall, broad-shouldered form. *John.* Even though the shadows bathed him, she'd know him anywhere. "Good evening, Mr. Goddard. I wasn't certain you'd come." She couldn't think of anything more erudite to say, since her tongue felt glued to the roof of her mouth and her feet wouldn't obey her brain's command to move.

"I've waited a long time for an invitation from you." He faced her, a grin parting his lips. Ice blue eyes twinkled with mischief in the dim lantern light while a smattering of raindrops sparkled like diamonds on the shoulders of his dark evening jacket and in the black curls that were slowly pulling out of the tamed style he'd chosen. "How have you been Miranda?"

She came alive hearing her name on his lips and moved onto the terrace a few steps. "Very nicely, thank you, Mr. Goddard."

"You know my name is John, and you've also made use of it in the past. You and I are well beyond the formalities."

"We are." Warmth swept through her body to ward off the chill from the drizzling rain. It had been a long five years since she'd last experienced his kiss, but she'd never forgotten. "I trust you've been well?" She devoured him with her gaze, wishing for one second it was her fingers and hands stroking along his lean, muscled form instead.

One heavy brow arched upward and gave a playful air to his rugged features. A dimple flashed in his chin, teasing in a square jaw ever so slightly shadowed with dark stubble. "My work keeps me busy enough, but I never could forget you."

He moved a few steps toward her. "I've spent many a sleepless night wondering what became of you."

"There isn't much to tell. I've been here in Surrey for the past two years." She started away as tingles rippled over her skin. He'd always affected her thus, and her traitorous body responded as if she was a green girl with her first beau.

"Why the invite now, when to the world you're still observing half-mourning?" He chased at his leisure, his steps slow and measured as if he had all the time in the world.

She quickly glanced at her muted grey silk gown with black jet trim. "If you must know, I am done with mourning, thank you. I simply haven't had new gowns done up."

"I see. Do you have specific plans in mind then with this party?"

"I do, actually, though I doubt they are the same ones you're thinking of." *Did* he think of her as he claimed?

"Oh?" His voice flowed through her, smooth and thick as the most luxurious chocolate.

Miranda stifled a shiver. Why couldn't she control her reaction to him? It was absolutely imperative she do so, for if he married her cousin, they'd be together for family occasions. It wouldn't do to let lingering desire have life. She rubbed her hands up and down her arms. Still, a few seconds of hesitation hovered between them. "Yes. It is my intention that you'll think my cousin favorable and the two of you will strike a match." Another twinge besieged her heart at the utterance. *Silly woman.*

"Ah, taking charge of everyone's lives around you." John followed her across the terrace. "I have no intention of falling for your machinations."

"Then why are you here?" Her footsteps slowed. "Are you nosy like all the rest, come to gawk at me for your amusement, to see if I've managed additional scandal?" She hadn't thought he'd come to her sanctuary just to be mean.

"Never, though one does have to question why you invited such people to your party if you feel thusly about them."

Heat sank into her cheeks. "The alternative of shunning the powers-that-be would ultimately lead to more problems."

"Still, I am surprised you followed even that protocol." He shook his head. "I'm here for you."

A thrill shot down her spine. "For me? Ah, you must mean because of my party." Surely that was why he'd come, yet she couldn't quiet the flutters in her stomach.

"There is unfinished business between us. I think you know that." He continued his pursuit while she retreated. "I am curious perhaps. We've danced around the heat between us long enough. I'm interested to know if the embers remain."

Miranda took her train in hand to prevent tripping in her haste to keep distance between them. "Why?" Some of the doors leading into the drawing rooms had been closed, keeping the terrace semi-private and the rain out. Music and conversation spilled into the night, but she paid it no mind, not while her virile companion stalked her with delicious intent.

"Why not? Also, I'd like to know if you're truly misfortunate or are you really Misfortune's Lady? It makes all the difference, you see."

What an odd question. "That depends on the subject." Oh, he was sly. In that one moment of heated promise in his voice, she knew she'd never match him with Annabelle. He was too big, his presence too all-consuming, too much for her young cousin to tame. He awakened the old excitement inside her, made her crave the abandoned wanton she'd once been—the woman who'd enjoyed all the benefits of sexual bliss married life had brought.

Perhaps I *should try and take him on...*

"With John, the subject is always the same. It's been you for as long as I've known him," a different voice echoed from the darkness. Another man materialized from the shadows. "Years ago, you made an impression on him he hasn't been able to shake."

Her heart lurched. "I'm not certain I want to discuss such private matters with a man I don't know." Miranda forced moisture into her dry throat. What madness was this, alone on the terrace in the company of two men who talked in circles?

"Ah, if that is your only reservation, allow me to introduce my friend." John gestured and the second man stepped closer into the golden light from the windows. "This is Mr. Richard Howick, back on England's shore for a respite from the War Office's demands. He's rather a celebrated spy in certain circles."

She nodded at the newcomer. He was the other man she'd wanted for Annabelle, except... Miranda worried her bottom lip with her teeth. Mr. Howick skulked in shadows, and from John's description, the man had a dangerous job that would take him from England for long stretches. Perhaps he wasn't the right choice for Annabelle either. *Bother. Why did matchmaking need be so difficult?*

"And a rake in others," the man added with a wink.

"Ah." Her pulse tripped into double time. Mr. Howick had no business being so mysterious or attractive, yet she couldn't resist engaging him in conversation. "Mrs. Miranda Ellis Mason Craythorne." Thinner than John, but equally masculine, he sported short, light brown hair and a completely different build. Whereas John had a good three inches of height, the other man seemed leaner, as if he were constantly in motion and used to moving quickly. "Thank you for responding to my invitation." She dismissed explaining the real reason for her invite. No, Mr. Howick was not a candidate for Annabelle.

Richard grinned and stroked a forefinger along the thin mustache clinging to his upper lip. "I have no doubt we will grow close as the days go by." He threw a glance to John then focused his gaze on Miranda. "Is there a reason you've been widowed three times or are you truly a victim of luck?"

She eyed the men warily. "Does it matter?" Logic and self-preservation dictated she lead them both into the house and among the other guests, yet curiosity demanded she let the scene play out. *Why did they both seem on the prowl?*

"It does." John closed the distance between them. He slid an arm around her waist and drew her against his chest. "Perhaps the legality of it all dooms your relationships. Perhaps luck will only favor you if you take a lover."

Miranda had scarcely drawn a harried breath before Richard came behind her, his hands warm on her hips, effectively holding her between their two hard, male bodies. "Perhaps you need *two* men to head off any more misfortune because, after all, two of anything is always better than one."

Dear heavens, what have I fallen into? She stared into John's face. The crisp, clean scent of his shaving soap sent threads of need between her thighs, yet the spicier aroma that clung to Richard teased her senses and put her in mind of sumptuous bedrooms in the Middle East. "That largely depends on the viewpoint. If an antelope is tracked by two lions, that's not good for the antelope." *Which is exactly what I feel like.* Gentle rain seeped into her gown but did nothing to cool her overheated skin. If she stood outside much longer, the resulting mess would be talked about with more enthusiasm than if she'd dampened her petticoats.

"Does the antelope wish to be caught?" Richard whispered into her ear.

She fought a shiver. In the men's loose embraces, waves of need crashed over her. "I can ill-afford scandal, gentlemen. Perhaps we should join the party."

John's smoky chuckle caressed her. "It's only a scandal if we're caught."

"I've left that life behind." They had to understand she wasn't gossip's consort any longer. She enjoyed her staid life too much to damage it by a careless and dangerous flirtation.

He tucked the escaped curl behind her ear and his fingers lingered on her cheek. "Will you vanish into obscurity then? Give your vitality to the flora and fauna here?" John tsked. "That isn't the Miranda I used to know, the woman I lusted after."

"People mature." She couldn't help the tremble gliding through her body. Oh, how she'd missed a man's touch, if nothing else but to be reminded she was still young and alive. "There's nothing wrong with my life."

Richard pulled her backside flush against his front. "Except your bed is lonely and cold."

Oh, God, what would it be like to have them both in her bed? At one time she'd dreamed of having John's affections, but to know both of these men in carnal ways? A shiver shook her. She banished the inconvenient thought. *I want only to rusticate.* Yet her body continued to betray her. Her nipples tightened into buds that fairly screamed to be touched. "That is not something I wish to discuss—with either of you." She couldn't tell John that at times she cried from needing a man's presence, for no other reason than to be held in the wee hours of the night.

"Are you quite certain of that?" Richard's breath warmed her skin and the touch of his lips at her nape seared her.

"I..." Any moment now, Annabelle would come looking for her. What would her cousin think? A smidgeon of guilt assailed her. Who was she to enjoy the attention of two men when she'd asked them here to catch Annabelle's eye? Thoughts continued to whirl. Or worse, what would happen if she were found in such a scandalous tangle by Lady Underhill? "If we linger on this terrace, all three of us will have the devil to pay." Decadent, wicked heat chased through her insides and culminated between her thighs. It had been so long since she'd known a man's touch at her sex. How naughty to even contemplate having them both in her bed, but how could she choose between them as they seemed to come as a matched pair?

Regardless of what her body wanted, she firmly shoved away the delicious thoughts. *I am not that woman. I do not need to revisit scandal.*

John's eyes twinkled. He ran the pad of his thumb along her lower lip. "Then, by all means, let us adjourn to somewhere more private."

"And close," Richard added while brushing his fingers along the side of her neck. "It would be vastly more superior to sipping lemonade and making dull conversation with those chits I glimpsed on my way in."

The words snapped Miranda out of the fog she'd fallen into. She broke from their combined embrace and backed away. Her chest heaved with the effort of remaining calm. Both men seemed inordinately interested in her bosom. "Gentlemen, I thank you for the interesting introduction, but I really must dash. I have guests waiting, and if my *good* luck holds, a business venture to embark upon."

John pinned her with a gaze that smoldered with enough heat to set her skirts on fire. "Our conversation isn't over."

She gained an open doorway and stumbled over the threshold. It was clear they wouldn't be put off so easily. "If you wish to talk with me, call tomorrow for tea." She glanced everywhere except at him—*them*. "I trust you'll be able to keep yourselves occupied this evening. I shall be much too busy to revisit this subject." Then, with her stomach in knots and the joy of the evening mired in confusion, she fled.

Chapter Two

The Honorable John Charles Henry Goddard, second son of the Earl of Ledford, paced the confines of Miranda's back parlor. He'd arrived some minutes ago, at which time her middle-aged butler had told him—in polite terms of course—to cool his heels until Mrs. Craythorne wanted to attend him. He'd agreed without complaint. For Miranda's good humor, he'd wait as long as it took. With a grin, he drifted to a window and clasped his hands behind his back. He could no more halt the excitement tightening his stomach than he could ask the sun to stop shining.

Damnation, but he'd fancied Miranda ever since they shared a passionate, impromptu kiss nearly five years before. Unfortunately, he'd had to leave that house party early. That same weekend, she'd met her second husband. John refused to miss another opportunity. He'd move heaven and earth to bring her to heel this time, except catching Miranda was much like trying to trap the wind. He'd rushed his fences with her last evening and no doubt spooked her with having Richard show his interest as well.

He blew out a frustrated breath. How to explain his penchant for enjoying the occasional threesome in the bedroom? He'd seen the flicker of fear in her eyes while on the terrace, but he'd also glimpsed the burn of desire. It gave him a modicum of hope.

I cannot worry about not winning her. Courting Miranda was his first priority. He'd never forgiven himself for leaving her alone during that house party or for introducing her to his friend Oliver, who'd become her second husband. John rolled his shoulders to alleviate the tension building there. He'd had plans to declare his intent that long ago weekend, yet Bow Street didn't wait for anyone's romantic aspirations, and he'd been summoned away. Had he gotten his man? Of course, he was good at what he did, but he'd also lost his woman.

Never again.

That had been the last time he'd pledged his services to the Runners. Once he'd realized Miranda had slipped through his fingers, he'd quit and started his own business as a private investigator, a man of the shadows, a gentleman of mystery, with plenty of time for his own pursuits. He simply hadn't wished to have his personal life rent asunder by Bow Street any longer. Too bad his decision hadn't come in time to pursue Miranda. Had he given his affections to other women in the interim? Of course, he wasn't a monk, and he enjoyed the warm comforts only a woman could provide. And now, a certain widow was his new quarry. Finally, they were both free of other obligations. He wouldn't fail this time.

John glanced out the window and his breath hitched. Down the lawn, Miranda moved among a muster of peacocks. She held a metal pail and every so often, she would scatter a scoop full of a grain-like substance over the ground for the birds to eat. His pulse kicked up. Should he join her outside or wait until she'd concluded her task and returned? As he continued his observation, one of the birds rushed her. It attacked the hem of her lavender dress, tugging with its beak. Miranda, in the process of yanking the fabric from its grasp, stumbled and fell on her bottom. The birds attacked the pail, swarming and seething around it in a blue-green mass until he could hardly make out Miranda's form. Among the iridescent tangle, one lone white peacock strutted, apparently not eager for the food like the others.

With a snicker, John turned away. Perhaps he'd wait until she returned to the house. After all, he'd just purchased this jacket and had his boots recently shined. Those birds were decidedly determined and most likely very messy.

As time dragged on, after Miranda had long quit the area outside and hadn't showed herself in the parlor, John's amusement turned into simmering annoyance. If she thought to leave him here for hours, she could think again. Their association wouldn't languish in the annals of history, not when he had breath in his body. He shot to his feet and quit the parlor. Halfway down the hall, he spied the butler.

"Excuse me, my good man, but could you please point me in the direction of Mrs. Craythorne? I'm rather in a hurry to speak with her."

"I believe she is feeding her birds in the conservatory—"

John didn't wait for the rest of the sentence. Knowing Miranda was in the same house, yet not able to see her, set his nerves on edge. *I've wasted enough time. A warren of hallways will not delay me.* He strode down the hall and turned a corner before he realized he had no idea where that room was located. By the time the butler, with his chin held high, led him down another passage, John regretted his hasty departure. Running off with more enthusiasm than sense would never win Miranda's heart. He took a deep breath then blew it out and wished for calm.

As a matter of course, both he and the butler arrived at the conservatory. Before the man could announce John's name, John had plowed through the open doorway. The butler harrumphed but left.

Noise burst upon John's consciousness. He gazed at a golden cage perhaps three feet by three feet, in which small parakeets fluttered. At least twenty of the colorful birds flitted back and forth, alighting on branches and perches, chattering to their heart's content. The tropical atmosphere brought on by the afternoon sun pouring through the floor-to-ceiling windows crowded his senses. Potted plants of all varieties, heights and widths occupied the windows and corners and crowded about the groupings of delicate, white-painted furniture. Above everything, this room screamed a "female's retreat." Beyond a doubt, Miranda spent the bulk of her time here, for books decorated the tabletops, and near one of the upholstered chairs, a sewing basket waited with a piece of embroidery draped over the arm. He narrowed his eyes. Why did she persist in hiding away in the country? Surely this sort of life wasn't enough to satisfy her.

For a few seconds he watched the blur of yellow, green, sky blue, white and lavender budgerigars. Once he put their tendency to cover everything in their path with pinfeathers and defecation from mind, they instilled calm in him. Would they alight on his fingers if he stuck a hand inside the cage? Would they bite? He shook his head. *I'm not here to fall victim to avian charms.*

"Miranda, I assume you were aware I waited for you in the parlor?" He paused near a potted palm tree as tall as his six-foot frame. His gaze landed on her, standing in front of a large, gilded cage hand-feeding a snowy white cockatoo. Its large talons curled about a perch, and it held a grape in its sharp, black beak. Why did she gravitate toward birds?

"I knew you were hanging about, yes." She didn't turn, merely continued to offer bits of fruit and nuts to the bird. "However, my birds take precedence, no matter who decides to drop in. They are on a schedule, you see."

"I beg your pardon, but why? I've never seen so many birds in a private home before." He approached with caution. Would the bird rush out of the cage at him? "What compels you to care for them?"

"Why shouldn't I?" Miranda deposited the remainder of the treats at the bottom of the cage. When the bird's yellow crest raised and it squawked and bobbed its head, she withdrew her hand then closed and latched the door. "Birds are lovely companions. All they want from life is food, fresh water and to have the paper lining their cages replaced every once in a while. Above that, they need affection and return it in their own way. They have no ulterior motives nor do brown studies affect them."

"And the peacocks?" He fisted a hand. She still hadn't faced him. Had he mistaken the desire in her eyes last night? *Not hardly.* He was trained to pick up much subtler clues than that.

Miranda glanced over her shoulder and smiled. Her blue-green eyes, the color so like the peacocks' feathers, twinkled in the sunlight. "When I traveled all over England with my first husband, he was given a pair from the Marquis of

Chatham on a visit. Apparently, the pair got on together well, for now my flock has grown to nine."

"From the parlor, I watched you feed them."

She turned fully then led him toward a settee and gestured for him to sit. A few pinfeathers clung to the front of her muslin dress, but a quick brush of her hand sent the feathers floating to the floor. Once she perched on the edge of the settee, he sat. "Yes, they have a rather particular diet, which I grind myself with a mortar and pestle."

"Indeed?"

"Yes. They receive a mixture of termites, ants, plants, flower petals, and seed heads. Sometimes, I'll treat them and include scorpion or locust parts, whatever I can procure from my contacts in the shipping industry."

"I see." John struggled to keep his neutral expression in the face of the unsettling information. He didn't care one whit for the dietary concerns of birds. "They're all descendants of the original pair?"

"All but three. A male and a female came from the wild and decided my flock was a nice enough group." She retrieved a folded towel from a tray in front of her and wiped her hands. "They stayed. I'm hoping they'll nest soon."

"And the ninth?" He sniffed and caught a delicate whiff of lemon juice and a more stringent note of a cleaner from the towel she used.

"That would be the white one. I've named him John."

John's stomach lurched. "I beg your pardon?" Had she named the fowl after him? Why couldn't she have gifted a falcon or some other bird of prey with his name?

"His name is John, and yes, he does bear your name. There's a reason for that." A playful grin lit Miranda's features. "He flew in during a rather harsh bout of rain a month ago. He struts around the lawn with his plumage on display, but none of the females in the muster take notice. Perhaps they think he's all blather."

His pulse increased. "What an unfortunate state of affairs." Hellfire and damnation, was that what she thought of him, that he was all talk or pompous even? "Perhaps he is merely determined to attract the eye of the female he's desired for a long time, yet she's doing her best to ignore him." Since she'd recently named the peacock John, did that mean she thought of him often?

"Stranger things have happened." A tinkling laugh broke from her throat. "There is a wild peahen that lives not far from here. She occasionally comes by to investigate, but remains on the outskirts of my property. She doesn't seem particularly bothered that she's alone. Perhaps she's not interested in being mated, or perhaps she's biding her time and observing John's showy ways to see if he has any substance."

A delicate shrug lifted her shoulders. "I, for one, am not worried, though I do spend much time studying her habits. I'd like to see her matched with him. If they had a clutch of eggs, those peachicks would be beautiful."

His thoughts tumbled over each other faster than he could fully realize them. Was that a hint she watched *him*, and consequently had considered having children with him? The short answer? Probably not, and why would she? He'd only just come back into her life. Miranda remained an enigma.

When she didn't offer up further conversation, he rushed to fill the silence. "It's interesting you find parallels in the bird's life and your own." He crossed his legs at the ankles while he raked his gaze over her person. The sun's light brought out a reddish sheen in her blonde hair. How he'd dreamed of her luxurious mass of curls, imagined what it would look like gracing his pillow or feel like sliding over his skin. His cock twitched. He'd waited long enough. If Miranda wished to lead him a merry chase, so be it. Assuming she wished for an association with him. One way or the other, he'd win her hand. "It's encouraging you've remembered me enough to carry over my name to the peacock."

Miranda said nothing, merely stared at him with wide eyes and a faint smile that set his insides aflame.

He flicked his gaze to her rose-colored lips—lips he'd spent endless minutes dreaming of. God, she was not created to be alone. She was too kissable for celibacy. The urge to discover why she chose country retirement grew strong. He cleared his throat. Too many thoughts about kissing Miranda would distract him from his mission. "Why do you choose to rusticate here? You used to be so vital, so mischievous, always willing to dive into scandal and set the tabbies' tongues wagging."

"I like to think I still am all three—just in a different way and to a different set of living things."

Damn, we're back to the blasted birds. Though the domestic side of her when she cared for the birds played havoc with his heart and drove home her nurturing spirit, he longed for her wanton side and wished to coax a tiny bit of that back out. *I need to remove her from this house.* "I am not here to discuss your penchant for becoming chatelaine to the avian world."

"Why *are* you here, John?" His blood sang to hear his name on her lips. One of her blonde eyebrows arched. "I must say I was shocked that you'd actually responded to my invitation, and even more so when you showed an interest in me instead of my cousin."

"Although I figured your party was to introduce your relative to marriageable bachelors, my interest in you isn't new. As I told you last night, I really *am* here for you." It mattered not to him in which personality—domestic marvel or Society's scandal maker—she wished to come with as long as she did.

"Oh posh." She waved a hand.

"You are still very much attractive, and I intend to win your heart this time around before someone else lays claim to you." A sense of smugness descended upon him at the statement. He had nothing to lose from free speaking.

"I see. Do I have no say in this?"

"Of course, but perhaps I'm getting ahead of myself once again." He reined himself in. *I must call upon my patience, else she'll spook like her birds.* Dash it all, he did not want her to fly away again. "Forgive me. I'm out of practice for courtship." Sexual liaisons he'd had, but courting wasn't his strong suit.

Worry lined her expression and was gone before he could study her closer. Doubts raised their ugly heads, mocking him. If that kiss at the house party years ago had affected her, why had she gone on and married twice over instead of seeking him out or sending a carefully worded letter even?

"Where is your friend? Somehow, I expected you'd both arrive together today and renew your pursuit from last evening, unorthodox though it may have been."

"I'm quite certain there will be more of that." Heat shot through his body. Had she enjoyed their flirting? "Richard is his own person. He does what he pleases when he pleases and refuses to tie himself to anyone or anything. Like me, he's taken rooms at one of the inns in the village." John shrugged, and then feeling as if his nerves would jump from his skin because of her close proximity, he stood in favor of pacing the room. "I suppose Richard's restless spirit is a result of his being a spy and always pretending he's someone else."

"We all have dual personas at times." She glanced at her birds then returned her gaze to him. "While Richard is busy obtaining international secrets for the War Office, how are you passing the time? The last I'd heard of you, you'd set the Runners on their ear with your talent and skill."

Quickly, he squelched the urge to preen and thereby further her analogy of him and the peacock. "Yes, well, Bow Street has had to get along without me for the last five years. I have been spying on the private citizens of England for anyone who wants their secrets and who will pay my fee."

"Why the change?"

He approached the budgie cage. "This occupation allows me more freedom than the Runners did, more freedom to pursue what—or who—I want." When he chuckled, the birds flew to the other side of the cage with more than a few squawks of umbrage. "Richard and I aren't all that different, yet we have very diverse goals."

"That may be so, but do you both work to preserve your bachelor state?" Miranda rose. "Or perhaps you both enjoy finding a new and exciting opera singer or Incomparable to grace your arm? You were never without a young female by your side. And while we're on that vein, do you two often share women, or is that a new and alarming proclivity?"

Here was the opening he needed. "Do you perceive it as alarming, or is it a new adventure you'd dearly love to embark upon?"

She twirled a lock of hair around her forefinger, the personal fidget she'd always had that meant she was either agitated or nervous. "It is too early to tell."

"Ah." He suppressed a triumphant grin. At least she'd thought about being with him and Richard. Now he merely had to apply his consummate charm and win her. The rest could be worked out at a later time. "My need for a *ménage a trois* only shows itself at random intervals. It's there to enhance relations between a specific woman and myself, and no, this proclivity as you call it, does not occur with every woman." John frowned. Over the years, when she'd been in relationships with other men, he'd felt the urge to occupy his time with bed sport, yet he'd still grown bored. None of those women compared to what he imagined being with Miranda would be like. "I suppose indulging in a threesome doesn't lend itself well to making plans for the future."

Why, then, did he hope a *ménage* with Miranda would be exactly that?

"Then why do it at all? Is one woman not enough for your enormous ego, or do you fancy your prick is so large you need two women to satisfy it?"

He laughed. "My dear, I do not need two women, and yes, I rather think my member is large enough to pleasure one, but you will be the ultimate judge on that score." God, how he'd missed exchanging banter with her. "I've never bedded two women, though there have been times I've thought about it."

"Lack of follow through, then?"

He narrowed his eyes. "Hardly. Finding one woman who wants the scandal is difficult enough."

"And Mr. Howlick?" One of her eyebrows rose.

"Richard has his own reasons for joining in, and you will need to ask him if you're curious."

"I shall when next I meet him. Are you two... intimate with each other?"

John shook his head. She was asking questions. This was a good sign. "No. Both Richard and I are friends, but the relationship is limited to that. In the bedroom, both his attention and mine are focused solely on the woman's pleasure."

A flash danced through her eyes. "It's all very fascinating. I wonder how you two came to such a pass to begin with. When I met you years ago, I had no idea your interests were so varied or complex."

"The need hadn't shown itself until after I'd lost you to Oliver." He frowned, not wanting to revisit that subject. He'd spent a fair amount of time with a fair number of women in the hopes he'd forget Miranda, but to no avail. With that one, long ago kiss, he'd been well and truly caught. Indulging in an occasional *ménage* had given him the opportunity to focus his attention exclusively on the woman in the hopes of forgetting Miranda. It had done no good. "I'm certain Richard will be along later. Then we'll sit down and regale you with the stories if you wish." As much as he wanted to rush to her side, take her into his arms and finally claim the second kiss that had tormented his dreams, he stood his ground. Not yet. Right now, he needed to show her his softer side. "I cannot speak for Richard, but I'm ready to put my bachelor days behind me."

"A little difficult to do if you crave a threesome."

"Yes, well, where there's a will, there's a way, or so I hope." *Please, God, let circumstances with her be different.*

"Not to mention such a carnal complication would cut into the lifestyle which usually follows marriage or courtship." When he cocked an eyebrow, another round of laughter broke from her throat. "Never say you're serious about setting up your nursery? I didn't think you'd envisioned yourself with a family. And if you are and the woman in question does find herself with child, how would you react not knowing which man fathered the child?"

"To me, it wouldn't matter, especially if the three people involved are committed to the relationship.

Miranda laughed again, only this time, the sound was a bit on the tight side. "I cannot fathom how you settle with this."

"Why does that amuse you?" Her response didn't bode well for a courtship.

She once again twirled a curl around her forefinger. "It doesn't fit in with the John I used to know. *That* John never appeared in public without a beautiful woman in tow and would never consider wanting a family enough to perhaps consider making such a large life change."

"This is true, but then, I guess I was a fine enough candidate for you to attempt to match with your cousin." He wanted to crow with laughter when a blush seeped into her cheeks, but he kept his composure. It wouldn't do to get too confident.

"Don't be more of a nodcock than you can help, John." Her lips twitched with a smile. "While I did initially think to match you with her despite your history, our conversation on the balcony changed my mind. However, I do hope your past is indeed in your past."

John's pulsed rushed in double time. "Perhaps the man I used to be had no idea what he wanted from life. That man did things for the recognition and the fame and even temporary fulfillment. All are rather empty endeavors without someone to share them with."

"I wonder." Her skeptical expression sent threads of fear into his heart, leaving his hope cold.

"A man can change as time goes on. Women, too."

"This is true. Although, I can't help but think, is it your father who wants grandchildren? After all, you aren't getting any younger."

His guffaw sent the budgies into yet another tither. He ignored them. "I am the spare, remember. Father hasn't seen fit to muck about my affairs like he has my brother's. No one cares what I do now that Geoffrey has secured the line." He rubbed a hand along his jaw. "My wish to be leg-shackled and have children is mine alone. At times, a man's business makes him stare his own mortality in the face and realize life is more than the job."

"How very mature of you to say so, but yes, it is a bothersome fact of life. Once Oliver died, I remember being well aware of my own expiration chances." Her blue-green eyes twinkled. "I hope you weren't in grave danger recently and that's what precipitated this change in mood, for if you were, that wish could just as easily vanish like the mist. I'd rather not fancy myself a convenient fix to a temporary craving."

"Absolutely not. I stand firm in this regard." When the cockatoo screeched, he darted a glance to it. What secrets did that bird hold from all the time she'd spent with it? It regarded him with beady black eyes that made him shudder. Was the key to winning her heart tolerating her feathered friends? "As I said before, a person can change. I certainly have. Or take yourself for example."

"How so?" A guarded note had crept into her voice.

"You married Oliver shortly after that house party, then wed again once his mourning period passed. Obviously, you were seeking something you'd not achieved as of yet." How gauche to mention her deceased husbands, but he tried to prove a point. "Would you not consider marriage again if the right man came along?"

Shadows clouded her eyes and completely banished her earlier levity. "I am not certain I want to find myself in the wedded state again, let alone subject a man to my misfortune."

"You don't have bad luck. Fate, it would seem, conspires to keep you from the happiness you deserve. It's certainly managed to throw my path far astray at times."

She pinned him with a glare. "Make no mistake, I was happy in all three of my marriages, and I am happy in my widowed state. One doesn't need to be wed in order to have a full life."

"This is also true, yet I suspect you're not telling me the whole truth."

"Then that is your issue, and I'm not of a mood to share secrets with you today." She crossed her arms beneath her breasts. The soft material of her dress pulled taut over her chest and fired his imagination. What would her breasts feel like in his hands, in his mouth, around his cock as he thrust between them?

"Poor Miranda." John shook his head. "I didn't mistake the desire in your eyes last night. I know you're far from satisfied in your domestic role here." He closed the distance and held out a hand. "I'm of the opinion that finding a person you can get on tolerably well with won't kill you either. It's not a bad omen to want more. For the moment, let's just say I'm offering companionship in these visits. Only time will tell what else comes from them."

"But, I thought you wished to court me?"

Was that disappointment in her expression? He winked and kept his excitement in check. He'd court her, all right, but he'd do it with finesse and charm that she couldn't pass on. "I fancy a drive in my curricle. Will you accompany me?"

"That largely depends on what else you intend to do while on a drive."

He chuckled. Oh, his Miranda had a sharp mind, but in the end, he'd outsmart her—and his career had taught him patience. "It's hard to tell, but seeing as how it's a nice day, perhaps I'll leave it up to fate." He wriggled the fingers of his outstretched hand. "I cannot be held responsible for anything untoward that happens, especially in the face of your country beauty."

"Naughty boy. See that you mind your manners." A grin curved her lips. "I'm smart enough not to be caught in your flirtations." She unfolded her arms and slipped a hand into his. "After all, scandal and I parted ways years ago."

"I am truly sorry that you think so." He pulled her hand through the crook of his elbow, inordinately pleased when she didn't attempt to stop his possessive behavior. Having her on his arm felt right. "The Miranda I remember fit scandal like a glove, but no matter. If you say you've quit that life, who am I to lead you astray?" He couldn't stop his grin as he escorted her from the room. He knew people, and he'd wager a year's salary Miranda secretly craved bit of the pleasure she used to know, and she most definitely needed a man in her life—possibly two. He'd let events naturally unfold. Eventually, she'd realize chasing excitement would be good for her, as was he.

Chapter Three

Miranda clasped her hands tightly in her lap. John had ushered her out the door and into his curricle before she could remember her gloves and hat or grab a spencer or shawl. Not that it mattered much. Her property sat to the southeast of Yorktown—or Cambridge Town depending on which political official you asked—well away from the village proper. No tongues would wag on her lack of decorum. Usually, she had no visitors, unless she'd specifically invited them. Without the accruements of propriety such as gloves, she felt vulnerable in his presence. The bravado she'd felt while in her snug conservatory deserted her. Here, out in the world, the task of protecting herself from gossips or stares loomed large. "If I may ask, where do you plan on driving? There's not much of interest between here and the village, and you're headed in the wrong direction if your aim is Farnham."

"The destination isn't important, for I have what I want at the moment—you by my side."

Oh, the veritable cheek of the man! "Then, from your own words, I'm yours only for the moment?" Not that they'd discussed a future.

"Smart as well as beautiful." He manipulated the traces with strong hands. The two gray-dappled mares kept an even pace down the lane. "I want you for far longer than that, but right now, my aim is to take in the air and enjoy the drive. Can't you just smell the first twinges of autumn?"

Surreptitiously, so she wouldn't give him the satisfaction, Miranda sniffed. Burning wood from stoves wafted to her nose as well as the scent of the wooded area they passed through and the more pungent aroma of fresh horse defecation. They were the smells of comfort, the scents she'd come to associate with her beloved home, but not for the world would she let him know that. "Not at the moment."

"Ah, perhaps your nose isn't the sense I need to charm."

"I meant what I said; I don't need a flirtation." She glanced at the hem of her dress, dismayed to see a dark streak of mud marring the light purple fabric. Of all the times to wear a soiled gown, it had to be in front of him. Inwardly, she groaned at her own vanity.

"That may be so, but you cannot deny the attraction between us."

"Humph." His confidence alarmed her even as it somewhat flattered. Had he been truthful when he said he'd wanted her all those years ago? A flutter tickled her insides. If he was indeed telling the truth, what would she do if he asked a direct question? She had to have some pride, after all, and even then, a dalliance would be all they could ever have.

"Were you always so stubborn, Miranda?"

"Perhaps." She thought briefly over all of her marriages. Eventually, she'd always gotten what she'd wanted—even if such things hadn't ended well.

"The wonderful thing about not having a destination in mind is you can stop anywhere along the way and change your circumstances." John tugged on the reins. Once the curricle drifted to a halt, he threw the brake and wrapped the traces around the lever. Then he shifted on the seat to face her more fully. His eyes were such a light blue in the afternoon sun they were almost clear, but they gleamed with unmistakable intent.

"My circumstances are not in need of changing." She squirmed. Being so close to him, with his presence surrounding her and his clean scent teasing her nose, her heartbeat increased. The heat he'd started last night flared. She'd been serious when she said she wasn't looking for another marriage. He didn't deserve her ill-fate no matter how much her body urged her to encourage the flirtation. "Perhaps you should take us back to the house."

"I think not." Humor wove through his voice. "You're a terrible liar, Miranda."

Despite her intention to ignore his charms, a tremble moved through her from the way he murmured her voice. Would he indulge in bedroom talk or was he of the opinion beds were for sleeping and sexual relations only? "How so?" At least that vein of questioning would distract him from a flirtation and give her additional time to block his advances.

"Do you remember that house party?"

"The one where you left unexpectedly regardless that we had just shared a heated embrace moments before?" How could she forget? It had been the night she'd fallen hard for him, yet when he removed himself from the party without an explanation and in such great haste he hadn't bothered to pack his belongings, her infatuation had turned to annoyance that perhaps he'd played her for a fool.

Had he truly changed from the man who'd put his occupation ahead of everything else? Sure, he'd said he didn't work for the Runners any longer, but what if they were only pretty words and he was still as driven?

"Indeed. However, in parting I told you that before the party was out, you'd know the man who'd you'd next marry."

"I fail to see why any of this matters now." She had no idea why he would bring up such a trivial conversation. Who and why she'd married was no concern of his.

"You denied my statement and retired to the refreshment table with your friends. When next I heard of you, you and Oliver were thick as thieves with the banns read shortly afterward. The two of you had apparently enjoyed a courtship of barely a month." A trace of bitterness resonated in his words. "Though I was happy for you, of course, I couldn't help being jealous. Had I not left you with his company I could have claimed you. I could have stood in his place."

Heat crept into her cheeks. She'd indeed encouraged Oliver's advances in order to make John jealous. Only, he'd never come back for her and she'd grown to genuinely adore Oliver, mostly because he'd reminded her strongly of John. "If you were interested, you should have worked harder to win me, John." The revelation he'd desired her then awoke butterflies in her stomach. And now he was here, free, the same as she. Perhaps he'd been honest when he'd said he wanted her. Had she been too hasty in denying him? She forced a swallow to moisten her dry throat. If she agreed, it would only be a relationship outside matrimonial bonds for she wouldn't wed again. Could she be content to know him in a physical way but never be with him in the public eye?

"My work kept me unavoidably away." A muscle in his jaw twitched.

"It always did."

"I made steps to ensure it won't happen again."

Was that true? He'd always been so proud of his career. She reared backward and looked at him with new understanding. The Runners, of course! They must have been why he left the party in haste, and also why he'd ultimately left Bow Street. Just how deep did his feelings for her run, and did she want to probe? "How silly of me not to have realized it before now. You quit the Runners shortly after I married Oliver."

"Yes, but by then, you were wed. I refused to miss another opportunity at happiness due to the demands of Bow Street." His voice sounded terse and tight.

"I see." She nodded slightly. Had her marriage to Oliver made such an impression that he'd changed the whole course of his life? Her pulse raced. Five years was a long time, but she'd not forgotten him either. The revelation was slightly overwhelming. "Let's return to something you said earlier. Why do you think I am a liar? I need more information than a few hints."

He stared at her as intently as if she were a criminal he chased. A smile broke through his expression, a grin so charming and full of heat she felt the languid fire all the way down to her toes. "Ah, the age-old art of avoidance. Very well. Based on your response last night, I think you're in dire need of being thoroughly kissed."

"Pish-posh, what nonsense. I haven't been kissed for a couple of years now. Why ever would you think I need—?"

The rest of her protest died when he cupped her cheek. Seconds later, he pressed his mouth to hers, and her world dissolved into soap-scented warmth.

Oh, how wrong she was! She did need to be kissed, but only by him. Miranda moved into a more comfortable position to feel the best fit of his mouth on hers. This was so much better than that stolen kiss years ago. His lips cradled hers with strong, masculine perfection. The sweep of his heated tongue along the seam of her mouth was magical. The steady pressure of his fingers on her skin was divine.

He captured her face between his large palms, holding her still as he plundered her lips with quiet authority. When she gasped for breath, or to encourage him deeper, he darted his tongue inside to fence with hers. Hot satin explored her mouth as if he wished for nothing else than to imprint himself upon her soul. She met every questing thrust and then returned the favor by sweeping her tongue into his mouth to taste him. Men, though much alike in many ways, all felt and tasted different during an embrace.

John groaned, breaking the kiss. "A woman who responds like that most definitely has dreamed of being more than kissed." He slipped his fingers along the column of her throat, not stopping until they played down her spine, and he enclosed her in his arms. "You should indulge often, my dear."

It was ridiculous to deny he was right. "I might if you're the one asking." She couldn't resist tracing her fingertips along his clean-shaven jaw. "I also might be persuaded to keep you around if you kiss me like that again." Dear heavens, what had happened to wanting to stay away from scandal? Hadn't she learned that lesson with the deaths of her husbands? But oh, the touch of John's lips on hers had been heaven and reminded her why she adored being in a relationship.

"What poor form you two show, leaving me out of your intimacy."

Miranda startled at the sound of Richard's voice. She untangled herself from John's arms and craned her neck to see beyond the sweep of his wide shoulders. Need pulsed between her thighs with more urgency. Damn and blast but she wanted to explore the breadth and width of John if only to indulge her fantasies. Though she wasn't a stranger to the pleasures of the marriage bed, none of her husbands had ever set her blood alight or gripped her with the desire to drag them off into the woods.

And now she and John had been interrupted. She swallowed as memories of meeting them both on the terrace came rushing into her mind. Being pinned between their hard, male bodies had prickles covering *her* body. Her breath quickened. Perhaps she didn't mind the disturbance after all.

She stared at the other man. "Mr. Howick." Richard drew closer on horseback, and when he came abreast of the curricle, he dismounted with more haste and theatrics than caution. "What are you doing out here?" How could she resent his intrusion when he looked so dashing and wicked?

"Searching for you and John, of course. I called upon the house and was told by your frosty butler you'd gone driving." His tone conveyed affront.

Miranda grinned. Something about being in the two men's company caused goose flesh to race along her exposed skin. "Yes, well, Eppson has a tendency to be overly protective. He's been with me through all my husbands—the one constant throughout life's changes you could say." *Poor Eppson.* She imagined his frown of disapproval upon seeing yet another gentleman calling for her. He was of the opinion she needn't get involved with another man as the other three hadn't worked out.

"No matter." Richard's brown eyes danced with mischief. He planted one booted foot on a wheel spoke while a gloved hand gripped the side of the curricle. Every lean inch of him was primed for action. "Do me the honor of calling me Richard. I consider Mr. Howick my father, and he's the last person I'd like to think upon at the moment."

"Very well. Richard. Shall we all adjourn to the house?" Though it was highly unlikely anyone would come upon them in the lane, the real possibility someone would see her in their company made her stomach knot. She feared the disgrace more than being caught between them both once more.

"In a twinkling, my dear." He glanced at his friend and lifted a dark eyebrow. "We have a problem, Mr. Goddard, as your curricle only seats two, and I very much want to join this scandalous conversation."

"Then I shall rectify the situation." John grasped her waist and hauled her into his lap. As soon as she was secure, Richard climbed aboard and settled into her vacated seat.

Miranda's heart thumped heavy against her ribcage. Once again, they had her neatly trapped. "Gentlemen, this is neither the time nor place for a dalliance." John's arms around her held her steady while Richard snuck a hand beneath her skirt and chuckled when she attempted to squirm away. "Richard..." She left off with the admonishment as heat swirled up her limb. "Um..." Hadn't she wanted to deliver a dressing down? She couldn't think let alone form words as he moved his hand higher. The brush of his fingers over the back of her knee rendered her speechless and as limp as poached chicken.

John's laughter rumbled in his chest before it burst from his throat. Her nipples pebbled at the sound. They thrust against her shift and the rasping hurtled shivers down her spine. He put his lips to the shell of her ear and said, "Are you having trouble maintaining your mental acuity, Mrs. Craythorne?"

"She *is* rather flushed, my good man," Richard rejoined. He scooted closer, insinuating himself between her legs. "And looks good enough to eat."

"She is. I had a sip from her sweet lips, so please, indulge yourself." John brushed her breast with his fingers. "It's only fair for you to sample her as well."

A host of tingles ripped through her body. "Not here in the lane." No matter that she half-heartedly pushed against his chest, Richard slithered his free hand around her neck and urged her to him. "Richard—"

The moment her lips touched his, she was lost in a murky world of heady desire and white-hot lust. Richard's kiss was more intense than John's. Where John had taken care to woo and court her mouth, Richard's overture demanded her surrender. He didn't ask permission or wait for an invitation; he merely bullied her lips apart then shoved his tongue in, ordering her retreat.

Dear God, will he apply such forceful tactics in bed as well?

The thought was buried under delight the longer Richard kissed her. His mustache tickled her upper lip; the trace of stubble on his cheeks sent awareness into every pore. Simultaneously, John tweaked her already erect nipples.

Pleasure cascaded through her body. Moisture dampened her folds, even more so when Richard pushed his hand upward to caress her thigh.

When he broke the embrace, Miranda moaned, her chest heaving and her heart racing. Amusement lit Richard's expression. "Scoundrel." She wanted to smack the smug grin off his face, but she refrained. After all, she'd been a willing participant.

"I've been called worse." He chucked her beneath the chin. "Shall we adjourn to a more private place and finish this? I can guarantee you'll come to completion quickly by my hand."

Of that she had no doubt. Miranda narrowed her eyes. "I'm not certain. It's difficult to think around the two of you." She pushed him from her and then batted John's hands away. *What am I doing?* She licked her lips and tasted a trace of something sweet, like fruit juice. "Gentlemen, I thank you for the reintroduction to carnal excitement, but might I remind you I have no intention of moving this relationship forward?" Oh but how she longed to give in to their urging.

"Again, you are a terrible liar. Desire is evident in your eyes." John tucked a wayward curl behind her ear. "Sweets, don't mind Richard. I told you he has different goals than I do. Plus, he lives for the next thrill, a new level of excitement. He has no depth."

"I resent that remark." Richard's grin didn't waver. "Although, he's not far from the mark. Where my erstwhile friend has this nodcock notion of settling down to domestic bliss, I do not embrace that plan. I require merely carnal bliss to be happy."

As she listened to their easy banter, her heartbeat returned to normal and some of the frantic apprehension drained away. Both of them together might be a little much to take on. "What is your life's goal, Mr. Howick? Chase after anything in skirts?" She refused to be one of the masses to him.

"Ah, back to formalities, are we?" Richard's rumble of laughter churned the butterflies in her stomach. "Very well." He jumped from the curricle and stood looking up at her. "Becoming leg-shackled with a handful of brats is not on my agenda. I live very much for the moment and for the next pleasure, for the next intrigue, but I'm not so cold-hearted that I cannot care about a woman."

Her heart trembled. How novel to have two men in her pocket. Did he care about her though they'd just met? Miranda scrambled off John's lap and gained the relative security of the empty space on the seat. She dared to continue the flirtation. "And have you found such a woman who would willfully tolerate your cheek?"

He stepped back, his grin no less mischievous. "I'm beginning to think I have."

She gaped at him. He'd taken her bait without hesitation. *Dear heavens, what a tangle.* She was attracted to two separate men, both irresistible in their own rights. If that didn't land her on scandal's doorstep, nothing would.

With a fair amount of insolence, he touched a finger to the brim of his hat and strode to his abandoned mount that grazed at the roadside. "Shall we return to the house, or would you rather deepen our connection here in the woods? I have no preference for the results will be the same."

The man's daring knew no bounds, and neither, apparently, did his passions. It drew her farther down the dark path. Her jaw hung open, but she could think of no proper come back for his audacity.

Beside her, John unwound the reins from the hand break. "Enough, Richard. Let Miranda become accustomed to us both. She's been alone for too many years without knowing how deep her own desires have run." He glanced at her and his blue eyes darkened a fraction. "Perhaps it would be best if Richard and I left you alone."

Something akin to panic lanced down her spine. She desperately wanted to continue and find out how far she'd go. "No." Now that the first flush of heat had faded, her clarity had returned. "We will all return to the house and take tea like proper people. A relationship as you're proposing won't have a chance unless the three of us talk things out." Was she truly considering it? The thought made her tremble.

"Oh?" Pleased surprise infused John's inquiry.

"Quite frankly, I have questions, and I'm still very much in control. No man—not even you John—will enter into my life unless I give him permission." If pressed, she wagered she might capitulate. Yet, neither man needed to know that. "Do you both understand?"

When the men nodded, she suppressed a smile. They had to understand she wasn't a green girl to be bowled over by flattery and kisses. They would both need to work to woo her—and on her terms. Her pulse tripped through her veins. It had been a long time, indeed, since she'd been pursued, and she rather looked forward to the unorthodox arrangement. "Very well. Shall we continue on?"

Miranda concentrated on keeping her hand from shaking as she took a sip of her tea then settled the cup back on the saucer, which rested on a low table. Upon arriving back at the house, she'd told Eppson she and the men would take tea in the parlor. He'd murmured a question since she usually took the repast in her conservatory. She remained steadfast in her decision. The men had annoyed her with their high handedness with the curricle stunt. Though it had been pleasurable, if they wanted back in her inner sanctum, they'd have to earn her trust. Of course, she'd thoroughly enjoyed herself, but she also wanted to guide her own seduction. An abundance of caution might prevent her from being emotionally wounded later.

She refused to remember how wonderful their kisses had felt or how alive she became under their touch. Now was not the time. Those thoughts were for the night when she was alone and tucked away in bed, where she'd find bliss with her wandering fingers and think fondly of a man's caress from memories.

Yet, at the back of her mind, a little imp of doubt wouldn't stay quiet. *If you weren't so stubborn, your bed won't need to be empty tonight.*

Miranda cleared her throat. *I'm not ready to open my heart so soon.* For that's what would happen. It always did. She enjoyed a man's companionship too much. She set her gaze on John. His black curls ran riot over his head and a lock fell over his brow, lending him a rakish air. *I will not brush it back, no matter how my hand itches to do so.*

"After events of this afternoon, it's apparent I must set a few things straight." She transferred her gaze to Richard. He sat across the table from her and played with the emerald stick pin in his cravat, but the devilish grin that curved his lips remained in place. How wonderful it would be to feel his lips on hers again, but not now. "I am not a lightskirt, gentlemen, and neither am I a wanton. I've gained a fair amount of regard in Surrey, and I refuse to lose that for one afternoon of passion, no matter how tempting. So, why exactly are you here?"

Richard's chuckle was more like a purr in the quiet room. Gooseflesh washed over her skin at the sound. "What if it's more than an afternoon? I'm willing to accommodate your needs whenever—wherever—you might have them."

A shiver rushed down her spine. He'd be difficult to handle, but she was ready for the challenge. "Why must you push for a *ménage*? It is hardly proper, and highly scandalous. If caught, we'd all be compromised, and I have no plans to lose my hard-won respectability in this village to satisfy base urges. I've worked too hard and done too much penance for this life." Her voice caught as her husbands' deaths came to mind.

"It's no scandal if we're not caught." A wink accompanied his rejoinder, so much like John's earlier one. "I do it for the titillation, to increase the thrill and pleasure factor." His eyes twinkled. "Why enjoy one man when you—the woman—can enjoy two? Two men, intent on nothing except bringing you to release as often as you wish it."

Her stomach flipped. She peered at John beside her. "Is he always this bold?"

John rolled his eyes. "Unfortunately, yes. Hazard of the vocation I think." He cradled his teacup between his hands.

The fragile china seemed overwhelmed in his palms. Such strength, such power in those hands, yet when he'd embraced her, she'd felt cherished and protected. He'd handled her just as gently as he did the china. "For me, adding a third deepens the root relationship, but takes the individual performance pressure off. However, many times, it's more than that." He set his cup onto the table and then planted his hands on his knees. "Both Richard and I enjoy spending time with the woman, yet our case is much different than those you hear of in rumors."

"I've heard of many shocking things that go on in London." She cocked her head to one side. "Perhaps you should better explain our would-be circumstances."

"Much of the time, I will be tied to my work or out of the country." Richard leaned forward. He took a silver flask from an interior pocket of his jacket, unscrewed the top and poured a measure of amber liquid into his teacup. Once he replaced the flask, he sipped the beverage. "During these times, your affections will belong to John. For all intents and purposes, you and he can live quite a respectable life doing as you please and setting up housekeeping."

"Ah, and when you return to England?" She refused to look at John for fear of what she'd see in his face. Did he fully agree to the plan? Would she? How could she divide her heart between two men?

Richard's shrug was a thing of beauty. His form flexed and stretched as if he were a savannah cat. "I want the homey knowledge there's a woman waiting for my return and fretting over my safety, one who will welcome me with open arms and a warm bed, a woman who wants nothing more from me than pleasure and the occasional conversation piece."

"I see." Enlightenment dawned as he pinned her with a direct gaze. He actually did tell the truth. "But you'd rather not be tied down to a conventional marriage and everything that bond would entail."

"Exactly. It does not appeal to me, and besides, my occupation is dangerous. I would rather not leave behind a grieving family if something untoward should happen." Sadness veiled Richard's expression so contrary to the devilish image he tried to project that it gave Miranda pause. Moments later he blinked it away. What had happened to touch him so deeply? He drained his cup then set it on the table. "John has talked so fondly of you over the years I've been anxious to meet you. I feel as if you and I have already met. After that kiss we shared, I'm of the opinion we'll all get along famously between the sheets."

John cleared his throat. "Doing it up too brown, Richard, and very vulgar, aren't you?"

"I cannot help what I am. Besides, my effrontery makes you look all the better."

John grinned with the ease of familiarity. Obviously, they were fast friends. "While Richard is gone, you and I will be free to conduct our lives in whatever manner you wish."

"I understand Richard's need to jaunt off on the next adventure, but what of you, John? Will you seek greater pleasure elsewhere once you tire of me or see that your dream of me doesn't compare to the reality?" Miranda shot to her feet, more upset than she wanted to show. She rounded on them both, glaring. "Once a woman gives of herself physically, she cannot help but be attached."

John frowned. "I understand that, but—"

"I refuse to put my life, *my* pursuits, on hold in favor of being only a bedmate for you, John." But she wouldn't marry, so how would her refusal be fair to him? She bit her bottom lip, both out of frustration and to prevent it from trembling. Why was this so difficult? "At the end of the day, regardless of what sort of union we'd all have, how can I be certain you'd choose me over duty?"

"Miranda, darling, I gave you my word. You won't find a more honest man than me." John stood the same time as Richard.

Richard nodded. "This is true. He's disgustingly candid, which is why the more questionable cases fall my way."

John rolled his eyes. "My statements to you have been truthful. I want to court you, eventually offer for you, and if things go well, set up a nursery. When I make a commitment, I stand by it."

Her chest ached while she remained mired in confliction. After everything she'd already been through in this life, would it be madness to let two very determined men into her carefully constructed world? "I refuse to have my heart shattered if duty calls. One man is bad enough; two leaving me when obligation whispers would be my undoing." With her previous husbands, she had been very much a part of their lives and would often travel with them. In the case of John and Richard, neither held careers where that would be feasible. The worry alone would bury her alive.

Richard stepped forward and clasped one of her hands. "That is the point of a *ménage a trois*, my dear. To make certain the woman is well and truly undone."

Heat flooded her core and zipped along her nerve endings. She shook her head, slipped from Richard's grip and backed away. "Blast it, be serious for one moment." If they continued their dual assault, she wouldn't have a chance, and while there was a certain comfort in knowing two men desired her, she didn't want the eventual heartache they'd bring. "I'm not courting scandal, gentlemen. I'm not sure I could do what you're asking, no matter how tempting it sounds."

And she was tempted. Both men were pleasing to the eye and made her feel like flying with their kisses. What heights could she achieve while in their bed? They would fill the void brought on by living alone.

John pursued her across the floor, finally trapping her between a curio cabinet and the wall. "Do you miss your old life, the security of having a man by your side, someone to talk to?"

"I have my servants."

"That is not the same, love, and you know it. Don't you want a man who cares for you and wants to look after your well-being?"

Despite the heady offer, a laugh escaped her. "You mean a man underfoot, always needing to pursue his own interests, no matter how pleasing his courtship is?"

Richard sidled over, his hands behind his back. "Or a man under your body?"

Oh, bother. His cheek knew no bounds, but truthfully, she enjoyed his teasing. "I do miss some aspects of married life, but I refuse to subject another man to my foul luck—unless either of you wish to end up dead."

How to explain that she felt she'd been the unwitting cause of her former husbands' deaths? Marriage to her, for all intents and purposes, had been their doom.

John nodded. His eyes had turned somber. "I understand." He glanced at Richard then returned his gaze to her. "If you refuse the legality of it all, would you consider an affair? I won't lose you again, Miranda. If this is the only way I can be with you, I'll take it. As long as I'm nearby, I can continue my suit."

Her knees threatened to turn to jelly. In the face of Richard's blatant flirting and John's gentle words, she wouldn't have a chance. And hadn't she always wondered if she and John would get on? Miranda sighed. "Perhaps." Yes, she was the gazelle to their lions, but that didn't mean she couldn't give them a spirited chase. She licked her bottom lip and then grinned because she couldn't remain stern in the face of their abject hope. "You will have to charm and win me. After all, I am a woman first, and then a bedmate."

Despite her avid warnings to them, she couldn't deny the needs of her body or her curiosity. If nothing else, the dance would be entertaining.

"I do hope you comprehend my offer." Miranda pushed past her two suitors and swept to the door. "I caution you, be discreet, and gentlemen, the chase has begun." As confidence surged through her veins, she winked. "I trust you can both show yourselves out."

"Yes, but..." John shoved a hand through his hair. "Miranda?" Confusion rumbled in his voice. "What does this mean?"

It would be good for him to be off balance. "You may begin your seduction tomorrow. Call for tea as I have appointments the rest of the day." She escaped into the hall before the shaking in her limbs showed itself.

Good Lord, I'm actually looking forward to the flirtation. After all, that was one of things she loved about courtship, the intense wooing before passion won in the bedroom.

But will I survive with my heart and my independence intact?

Chapter Four

This delay is insufferable.

"Please tell Mrs. Craythorne I wish to speak with her as soon as she can manage. My business with her is quite pressing."

"I am her servant, Mr. Goddard, not her keeper. She does very much as she pleases, but I'll mention your request just the same. Perhaps next time, be certain you've made an appointment. Tea will be brought in when she arrives." The butler Eppson, true to form, bowed and exited Miranda's back parlor.

John took the news none too gracefully, as the urge to see Miranda had burned strong through the night, especially after their bout of kissing yesterday and her hint of the chase. Though he'd wanted to rush to her home at first light, he'd tamped the urge and found other pursuits to occupy his time—wondering which cravat knot she'd favor, determining what color jacket she might like and attempting to not to keep checking the time. Besides, she'd hinted she'd be busy for the bulk of the day. Taking her at her word would go a long way into putting him into her good graces, but the wait for tea had never seemed like such an eternity before.

Not for the first time since traveling to Surrey did John wish for his townhouse in London. His servants knew their station and place, and were not allowed to rule the household willy nilly. He gritted his teeth. This wasn't his home, and apparently, he and Miranda's viewpoints on operating households differed. John shrugged and set the problem from his mind. Domestic issues didn't matter overly much. He and Miranda work it out.

He blew out a frustrated breath but refused to sit. He had too much nervous energy to twiddle his thumbs. As it was, his anxiety wouldn't be contained and only pacing would do as thoughts of his hostess circled around his mind.

He'd spied the desire in Miranda's eyes yesterday, felt the passion when she'd returned his kisses. By the time Richard had joined them, John had been hard pressed not to take advantage of the situation and her right there on the public road. Yet he refused to rush into the relationship. Above all, winning Miranda came first, regardless of what his body needed. He wouldn't leave Surrey without securing her promise. On this he was certain; of every other aspect of making their relationship work—let alone adding Richard—he was not. If she absolutely didn't want the third, he'd have to invent some rather fancy explanations as to why he couldn't leave Richard behind. And what of his friend? It would completely break the man to be tossed into the wind.

John's stomach clenched. Worse still, what if she fancied Richard more than him? Could he walk away honorably and leave them to their life, or could he be content as their third but never having her full attention, always watching her and knowing that, again, he'd lost her affections to a friend? And what would happen once Richard went away?

He shoved a hand through his hair. *I need answers.* Beyond whisking Miranda off to his London address, he'd need to accomplish his task on her timetable. A sigh escaped him. Well, being a private investigator meant he'd learned to be flexible. He'd wait.

"If you're not careful, that brown study you've fallen into will scare away everyone around you."

He turned at the sound of Miranda's voice. She swept into the parlor followed by Eppson who pushed a tea cart. John gave her an easy grin he hoped would set her heart racing. "I apologize. There's much to ponder at the moment."

Neither of them spoke again until the butler quit the parlor.

Miranda gestured toward a pink upholstered settee. "Will you join me in taking tea, John? My work in the flower beds earlier has made me parched. I'd rather not enjoy refreshments alone."

Why did women feel the need to decorate with such flimsy furnishings? Once he'd dropped onto a dainty chair he feared would break beneath his weight, she busied herself with pouring out tea. When he took the offered cup from her and their fingers brushed, he nearly spilled tea all over his lap from the jolt of awareness the touch imparted. "I assume you do your own gardening?"

"Of small things, yes. I do so enjoy puttering, though if you ask Mr. Lovejoy. He'll say I'm more of a hindrance."

He didn't bother to conceal his interest as he swept his gaze over her immaculate plum-colored gown. The plain, square neckline did her bosom no justice. A single strand of pearls proclaimed her a lady—understated but with quiet authority. "You don't appear dirt-smudged."

"I should hope not." A tiny grin curved her kissable mouth. "When I spend time in the gardens, I'm there to cut flowers or gather produce from the vines. I leave the bulk of the work to Mr. Lovejoy—just as he likes it—and compliment him when appropriate."

"You're kind to everyone who comes into your life." He sipped his tea while attempting to ignore the awakening of his cock. "It's a trait I admire in you. Always have." Except when a person ruled their household with less than strong control, the servants tended to take advantage as had been evidenced with Eppson's cheeky attitude.

"Thank you. Nothing is gained in being ugly to the people around me when nothing except circumstances separates us." She nibbled on a honey cake then licked the crumbs from her lips.

John choked on a swallow of tea imagining what her tongue would feel like on his skin or her lips wrapped around his member. What he needed at this moment was a subject that would take his mind off the possibility of ravishing her quickly before her butler returned. "Will you ever entertain me in your conservatory? I must say this parlor doesn't mirror your vibrancy and loving nature." He gestured at the settee. "All of this is overly feminine, and quite frankly, it's cold and fussy, as if belongs to a woman used to having guests in but not enough to invite them to stay."

"This is true." She glanced around the room. "It was decorated to my sister-in-law's taste. Since I rarely use this room unless it's to entertain a quick social visit, I've left it alone.

It makes me sad, somehow, to come in here, and only serves to remind me that this house isn't mine."

"Which makes no sense as to why you've dumped me here—twice now."

"Poor John, will you pout?" She settled her teacup in its saucer and put the set on the table in front of her. "I'm simply not ready to share my sanctuary with anyone—let alone you. I must be able to trust someone completely before inviting them there."

"I talked with you there two days ago."

"Ah, but you weren't invited, were you?" She raised an eyebrow. "The more time you spend with me, the better your chances of earning my trust."

The back of his neck burned from her reprimand. "I apologize. While my vocation demands patience at long stretches, where you're concerned, I have none." He put his teacup near hers. "I'll be honest, Miranda. I can never forgive myself for letting Oliver win you." He wanted her to understand how deep his affections ran.

"If you had been as enamored as you'd said, perhaps you wouldn't have let the Runners rule your life." Only the tight clasp of her fingers in her lap gave away her feelings. "You never said anything of your intent, and when Oliver showed an interest, what was I supposed to do? At the time, I wanted to marry again. He was there. You were not."

Everything she said was the truth. The missed circumstance had been his fault alone, and back then, being a Runner had been more important to him than pursuing the love of his life. He'd learned from that mistake and wouldn't repeat it. Doubts once again flared. If Oliver weren't there, would she have chosen some other man instead? Did her penchant for enjoying a man's company extend to desiring Richard over him? He forced away his thoughts.

"I take full responsibility." As he thought about his next words, his jaw clenched, and he reminded himself to be as relaxed as he could while in her company. He'd gain nothing from appearing overeager. Honesty would work best. "I'll admit, when I learned of Oliver's death, though I was attached, I did wish to send off a missive to you, hinting at my interest."

"And you didn't, why?" The question was so soft, he almost missed it.

"Fear. Annoyance that you'd picked him in the first place. Insecurity that I'd misread our attraction." He shrugged. "By the time I'd extricated myself from my lady friend, the rumor mill churned out tales of your third courtship." His jaw tightened and he made a concentrated effort to relax. "I must reiterate this. I refuse to allow another man to swoop in and win your heart before I have the chance."

"Winning my heart will take more than a few heated, stolen kisses." Her blue-green eyes sparkled. "If you should need help with the match, I can guide you in the right direction."

Did that mean she wanted him to try harder? John cleared his throat. "Perhaps I'll ask for assistance later. Right now, I'd like to discuss your husbands." While it was true he'd loved Miranda for years, he knew very little about her life other than her perpetual state of marriage and widowhood.

"What would you like to know?" A note of wariness had crept into her voice.

What indeed? He wanted to ascertain why she was so haunted, why a silly curse seemed to bind her and prevent her from going into her future with confidence. Above all, he wished to simply ease her mind, tell her their alliance would be different. "Specifically, why do you believe you're cursed? Why do you think matrimony doomed those men?" He turned toward her, and his knee knocked into hers. A soft inhalation from Miranda was the only indication he affected her.

Shadows clouded her eyes. Her forehead furrowed. "It would appear I'm unlucky once the nuptial vows are read." Miranda stood and made her way to one of the windows but kept her back to him. "Had any of those men chose not to marry me, there's a chance they might still be alive today."

"Why? Life is hard. Your husbands all held occupations that weren't exactly staid, correct?"

"Yes." Miranda held her shoulders rigid, and her hands were fisted at her sides. "I married George when I was seventeen and just a wide-eyed girl out of the schoolroom. He was a novelist who wrote about the wonders of English wildlife. I thought he was quite worldly and fascinating. Noble, even." She leaned a shoulder against the window. In profile, she appeared lost in thought.

"That's not dangerous."

"Perhaps, but it was my fault he died. We were in the north, hunting down some sort of bird he desperately wanted to document. I'd mentioned I'd like to tour one of the castle ruins and he agreed. George never could deny me anything." A tiny, mournful laugh escaped her. "We set out walking. Soon afterward George caught a foot in a rotted board. When he struggled to free himself, the board broke and he fell into a well." She shook her head and crossed her arms over her chest.

"You don't need to continue if it stirs distasteful memories." John rose, unsure of what to do. If he went to her, she might rebuff him. If she accepted his embrace, she might not finish her tale and he wouldn't be able to resist her vulnerability. Once again, he'd race, overbearing and overeager, into the void.

"It's ancient history now." Her smile was frayed. "By the time I'd secured help, it was too late. He'd broken his neck besides maybe having drowned in the putrid water at the bottom." The tendons of her throat worked with a swallow. "I had nearly three years with him, but learned to love the outdoors as well as birds from his guidance. That's why I tried to make this place into a haven of sorts."

"It's a nice way to remember." A stab of jealousy lanced through his chest. The only way she'd remembered him was to name a vain peacock John. "His death was an accident, though. You didn't push him down that shaft."

"No, but if I hadn't wanted to see the blasted castle..." She wiped at the moisture in the corner of one eye. "I've made my peace with it, however painful the memory is."

"We all must move forward, even if the people we love don't come with us." He couldn't imagine how it felt to lose a spouse let alone three as she had. Yes, he'd hoped he'd have another chance with her when he'd heard about Oliver, but he hadn't wished to bear his friend ill will. From all accounts, Oliver had made her happy, and John couldn't fault him for that.

Miranda nodded. She stared out the window, presumably watching her peacocks. "Of course you know about my history with Oliver."

"Yes." His chest tightened with a trace of sadness. "He was shot at close range by a criminal's angry family member. That wasn't your fault either." John joined her at the window, standing just behind her. "You can't blame yourself."

"I can because that day I convinced him to let me attend a trial. At twenty-three I was enamored by human nature and all its facets. Oliver met so many interesting people through his relationships with the Runners. As a barrister, he'd been instrumental in putting many men into prison. A few times he'd been tasked with escorting a man to the Tower."

"Miranda—" He moved closer to her. He knew what came next and didn't wish her to remember if it would cause her pain.

"You wanted the story, John." She sighed. Her chest rose and fell with each breath. "If I hadn't been in the courtroom that day, if he hadn't leapt into the line of fire to protect me, he would still be here."

"But you would not." His heart aching for all she'd been through, John slipped his arms around her waist and pulled her backside against his front. For a few, fleeting seconds he reveled in how good her softness felt in his arms. "Forgive my frank assessment, but I'm glad you survived the madness." He remembered the day he'd gotten word. He'd been in the office with the other Runners celebrating with a friend who'd caught his latest target. He'd been devastated Oliver had met his end so viciously. When he'd wanted to comfort Miranda, he couldn't. It hadn't been the appropriate time and she had other people around her for that. Afterward, it seemed she'd vanished from London, perhaps choosing to keep people at arm's length after such a violent murder. By the time she'd resurfaced, he'd been attached.

She covered his arms with hers and held him tight. "Thank you." A shuddering sigh left her. "I suppose I enjoy men too much or had fallen in love with the idea of finding enduring affection. At twenty-five I married again. Poor Theodore had no idea what he was in for, but oh, we had such a wonderful time together. I learned the art of bantering conversation from him."

Another wave of jealousy swamped him. John tamped it as best he could. After all, *he* was here with her now, and it was only a matter of time before he'd win her. "Tell me of his livelihood." He pressed a kiss to her glossy hair. The scent of violets tickled his nose. It would always remind him of her.

"He was a member of the diplomatic corps as an ambassador of England to Spain and Portugal." She drew random patterns on the back of his hand with a finger. "I loved traveling with him. Many of the trinkets in the house are from those days."

"How did he die?" For the life of him he couldn't remember, not when it took all of his willpower to halt the urge to nibble a path down the slender line of her delectable neck.

"Food poisoning of all things. We were at a café in Barcelona. Theodore wasn't very adventurous in a culinary way. I dared him to try calamari." Her sigh seemed to come from her toes. "I declined to have any as I was already stuffed from eating more than my share of mussels." A shrug lifted her shoulders. "Again, I'd had a hand in killing a man married to me."

"That's not true." John turned her around until she faced him. "Yes, all of their deaths were unfortunate, but you weren't at fault." He put a finger beneath her chin and lifted her face so she met his gaze. "You're not cursed, Miranda. You're merely a victim of a fickle fate."

She shook her head, dislodging his hold. Her chin trembled. A mist of tears sparkled in her eyes. "I appreciate that, but there's always a niggle of doubt at the back of my mind that says otherwise." She twirled an escaped wisp of hair at her temple around her finger. "I'd rather not take the risk again."

"Does that mean you won't accept a proposal from me if I asked?"

"Yes." Her whispered confirmation warmed the skin above his cravat as she dropped her gaze. "I hope you can understand. You mean too much to me to take such a big chance."

Preliminary victory swelled his chest, but he refused to show it for fear he'd heard her wrong. "I had hoped you cared for me." Apparently, he was incapable of feigning disinterest around Miranda.

She lifted her gaze to his. "Of course I do, which is why whatever is between us can never go as far as marriage." She gripped his shoulders, stood on tiptoe and kissed his chin. "I'd rather conduct a discreet affair instead of burying another husband. At least then you'll be safe, and my heart won't break again."

John's spine tingled. She wanted the affair? It meant she'd thought of him in an amorous way, and it was more than he had this morning. His cock pressed against the front of his trousers. "Is it too much to hope my considerable charm has worked its magic on you already?" He slipped his arms around her waist and pulled her close. "It would seem I'm more potent than I'd anticipated."

"If you think so, and are gauche enough to mention it, you're more arrogant than I'd anticipated." Miranda smiled. She slid her palms up his arms and wrapped her arms around his shoulders. "Is that all you have to say, Mr. Goddard? Perhaps you're not as charming as you think."

"Touché, Mrs. Craythorne." John battled between the urge to protect her and the need to show her he wasn't worried about the alleged curse. Both of those emotions paled before his desire. "And no, I'm not nearly done." It'd been a long time since he'd been so excited about a woman, but his gut clenched as he lowered his head and claimed her lips.

Her lips were every bit as soft and pliant as he remembered. When he nibbled at the corners of her mouth, she responded in kind. Every lick, every trace of her lips, she mimicked. He groaned and settled her more comfortably in his embrace. The tickle of her fingers at his nape and in his hair heightened his awareness; the press of her breasts against his chest tested his willpower, but he didn't break the kiss. He swept his tongue along her bottom lip. When she gave a soft sigh in response, he pushed his tongue inside to tangle with hers.

The heated silk of her mouth fascinated him. He couldn't get enough. With every thrust of his tongue, he caught a faint taste of her tea. Each time she fenced with him his cock tightened. John pulled slightly away, his breathing ragged, only to trail kisses under her jaw and down the side of her throat.

Miranda moaned. "I've waited a lifetime to experience another kiss from you."

"I know the feeling, but we did share one just this morning." His pulse roared in his ears and throbbed in his temples. "You're so soft." He moved his hands to her hips and held her against his hard cock so she'd have no doubts as to his intentions. "I want you, Miranda. I have for so long." Unable to stay away, he licked at the spot between her collarbones then dared to drop kisses along the edge of her bodice. She trembled in his hold.

"I've hoped to hear you say that." The smile on her kiss-swollen lips was brilliant in the light streaming through the window. "John, I—"

The discreet clearing of a masculine throat near the door interrupted whatever she would have said. "Mrs. Craythorne, you have another visitor. The minister's wife requires an audience with you. Shall I show her in? She's waiting in the foyer."

"Bloody hell," Miranda muttered under her breath. She pulled out of John's arms and nodded. "That would be fine, Eppson, and bring another tea setting."

Damnation. John rubbed a hand along his jaw. He stared at her, somewhat mollified over their interruption since the hard points of her nipples poked against the fabric of her dress. "Shall I stay?" He couldn't wait to take those erect buds into his mouth. There was a chance, once the visit was over, he could salvage what they'd started.

"Yes, please, but if you wouldn't mind, will you wait outside? Maybe walk the lawn until she goes? I'd rather not risk her seeing you in the hall and asking untoward questions."

"I beg your pardon?"

"Well, I cannot very well hide you here. There's nowhere to conceal you, and I don't wish to have gossip destroy things between us before they can be properly started." A hint of panic shadowed her eyes. "You can go through the window, but do it quick."

What the hell? She wanted him to escape like a criminal? Run as if he'd done something wrong? Absolutely not, but when he glanced at her again and saw the pleading in her expression, his shoulders drooped. He could deny her nothing. He nodded. "Very well."

Miranda had barely regained her seat before Eppson showed Mrs. Stowe into the parlor. Miranda darted a glance to one of the large bow windows. The leaded glass panels were still open from John's escape. Not far over the lawn she caught the flash of his bottle-green coat before Eppson left and she was obliged to greet the local minister's wife.

"Welcome, Doris. I'm delighted you chose to visit me today." She waved the middle-aged woman to a chair opposite. Miranda remained seated so her guest wouldn't occupy any furniture that would allow her to see out onto the lawn. "What can I do for you?" Regardless of what she'd told John before, it took a great amount of effort to infuse a polite tone into her voice. She disliked nosy drop-ins and despised being interrupted.

"I wish I could say it was a leisure visit." Doris accepted a cup of tea and a plate of tea cakes from Miranda. She crossed her bony ankles and balanced the plate on a knobby knee her mustard yellow skirts did nothing to hide. "I'm here to discuss a certain happening that occurred at your party the other evening."

"Oh?" Miranda refreshed her own tea and took a sip. Outside on the lawn John approached the peacock muster. She bit her bottom lip. *Oh dear.* That would be a mistake. The birds, when threatened with a stranger, would try and run him out of their territory.

"Yes. I'm told, by a reliable source, you were seen in the company of two gentlemen, none of you with escorts or companions." She took a delicate sip of tea. "And what's more, you were very close to the men in a rather *scandalous* position." With her lips pursed and her sour expression, it appeared she'd tasted a lemon.

Miranda narrowed her eyes. "I see." She set her teacup on its saucer with a decided clink. "I rather think it un-Christian to gossip about members of the community."

The minister's wife huffed. "I came here out of concern for you, Mrs. Craythorne."

Ah, I must have hit a nerve if she's adopting a formal attitude. How many women had she gadded about with before coming here? "Nevertheless, I'll tell you I did visit with a couple of gentleman, but by no means did I indulge in a scandalous position with either of them." Flutters tickled her insides as she thought about the very outrageous things she could have done that night but had chosen to err on the side of caution instead.

"Be that as it may, I must tell you to curb any more inappropriate behavior." Mrs. Stowe ate two tiny honey cakes in succession as if she were starving. "I urge you to have some decorum. A woman your age and with your... experience... needs to remain out of the public eye."

"My experience?" A jolt shot down Miranda's spine while anger bubbled hot in her chest. "Are you referring to my marriage experience or something much uglier, Mrs. Stowe?" How dare the woman insult her in her own home?

Doris ignored the question. "Our young people don't need your sort of example, especially if you persist on matchmaking schemes."

Miranda opened and closed her mouth while she searched for something to say. "I beg your pardon?" It wasn't as if she'd run a brothel on her estate nor was she schooling young people on how to be scandalous. They'd find that out on their own.

"You see, you live so far removed from the village, it would be quite easy for you to be careless with decorum out here." The woman slurped her tea. "People could think the wrong things about you after a while. Who knows what sort of depravity has already occurred."

"Mmhmm, the wrong things. Please, tell me more." It wasn't that Miranda was interested in the vile woman's views. She wanted to buy time as John seemed to be in rather a big dilemma outside. As she listened to the drone of Doris's nasal voice, she observed the tableau on the lawn.

Poor John. Miranda pressed her napkin to her lips to cover a grin. As expected, the peacocks hadn't taken kindly to being approached by a stranger. John ran over the verdant green lawn with a few of the fastest birds right behind him. She honestly thought he'd escape. She even leaned forward on the edge of her seat, straining toward the outcome of the unfortunate footrace. He'd almost gotten away, except he tripped over something in the grass and tumbled headfirst onto the lawn. The peacocks swarmed him. Their agitated squawking and high-pitched shrilling calls reached her through the windows.

No matter how hard she tried, she couldn't see him through the flurry of birds in motion and bobbing heads. *I hope they don't damage him too badly.*

"Why, just at tea yesterday, Lady Underhill hinted you were in danger of being compromised if you let those two men continue to sniff around your skirts."

The idle prattle finally sank into Miranda's brain and yanked her from her concern about John. "What?"

Doris blinked at Miranda's exclamation. "Yes, dear. We're all afraid you'll be compromised if you continue to disregard the rules. I shudder to think what could happen if the news of your exploits reached the wrong ears."

Oh, I'm sure they'd like that. Imagine the months of gossip and reputation shredding. Miranda stood. "I have yet to do anything untoward, Mrs. Stowe. I'll thank you to remember this is my home and my property. Quite frankly, if I want to host a menagerie of wolves, take in orphaned children or make merry with gentlemen, I'll do what I please. It's not your place to tell me otherwise."

Outside, John had scrambled to his feet only to be chased back the way he'd come by the peacocks.

"Well." The minister's wife rose as well, her expression once more a sour affair. "There's no need to fly into the boughs with me, Mrs. Craythorne. I'm only passing on the warning. Society is watching. It's in your best interests not to anger the powers-that-be around Surrey."

Society can go hang for all I care. No matter how hard she'd tried, the tabbies would still talk, yet a wave of protection welled inside her for the men she had a budding affection for. Perhaps if society had such issue with her unorthodox predicament, it meant she was headed in the right direction. And why the sudden interest in her life now?

"Is there a threat attached to this warning as well?" Miranda was well past caring for civility. The powers-that-be consisted mostly of Lady Underhill and her cronies. Though Miranda had healthy respect for the baron's wife, she refused to let the woman intimate her. "Did Lady Underhill send you?"

If possible, Mrs. Stowe's lips pursed tighter. "She suggested I come talk to you, yes." Doris folded her hands at her waist. "The baroness wields a fair amount of influence around Surrey. Please have a care."

"Why?" She didn't like the false empathy in the other woman's tone.

"Matchmaking might be your calling, but I must warn you that no one would entrust their future happiness or that of their marriage-aged children to a wanton who might steal their prospects somewhere down the line." Her laugh sounded forced and brittle. "My dear, it's no secret you have a voracious appetite for the males. You've been thrice wed."

Stuff and bother! It was time to ask the vile woman to leave her home. "This is *my* warning." Miranda strode to the door. On the lawn, John had managed to leave the muster behind and headed toward the house. She needed to remove the minister's wife from the area as soon as possible. "You tell Lady Underhill that if she takes issue with me or how I run my life, she's more than welcome to come here and discuss it with me personally. Otherwise, your concern isn't warranted. I'm widowed, not a debutante. I cannot be ruined, and I don't plan to marry again. I don't have a voracious appetite for men, but since I am a woman, I do enjoy being courted. It's not a crime." She paused briefly for breath. "Plus, I enjoy matchmaking. Nothing you can say will deter me from helping those wishing a hand in romance." Except if she were to be tossed from Surrey society, there wouldn't be invitations issued and thereby no opportunity to help lovelorn young people. Though her heart trembled, she pushed the thought away. She could worry about that later. She stared pointedly at Doris then at the door. "Will there be anything else, Mrs. Stowe?"

"No, I don't suppose there will be."

Miranda maneuvered around so the other woman would have no need to turn back and thereby see John coming closer. "I thank you for the visit, and please, do come again if there are any other questions you think I can help you with." She resisted the urge to bodily shove the woman from the parlor. "Eppson will gather your things and show you out. Good day."

No sooner had Doris's skirts cleared the doorframe than John climbed back through the window. Miranda rushed across the room toward him, not bothering to stifle her laughter. "Oh, you poor thing. Are you hurt?"

John brushed ineffectually at the grass and dirt on his jacket. One of his sleeves was torn beyond repair. Bird feces, pin feathers and mud streaked his once-immaculate ivory breeches and his hair stood in disarray all over his head. "Only my pride is wounded." He plucked a leaf from his hair and flicked it to the floor. "It would seem your birds do not take kindly to having their day interrupted."

"It takes them time to trust." Another trill of mirth escaped her. "I truly apologize." She fingered the ripped fabric all the while her ribs ached from stifling a peal of hard laughter. "Is there anything I can do?"

His expression suggested she should go jump into the nearest lake, but he politely rejoined, "No thank you. I shall return to my rooms for a bath, a bourbon and to implore my valet's forgiveness. This was his favorite coat."

She couldn't figure out if he was affronted that his clothes had been ruined or because the birds wouldn't accept him. Miranda patted his arm. His muscles stiffened beneath her hand. "Come riding with me tomorrow morning. Then we'll have breakfast together. It's the least I can do."

"I'd enjoy that." He nodded. "I'd rather not encounter the peacocks again, but I will if making friends with them will win your heart. Good day, Miranda." With his back ramrod stiff and his broad shoulders squared, he quit the parlor, the impact of his determined exit lessened by the fact a peacock feather was stuck to his rear end.

She stared into the empty space he'd just vacated. A tickle flowed through her heart, cleansing away any ill will Mrs. Stowe had brought. If he'd be willing to offer himself up to the birds again, his intent to win her must be serious. Once she was sure he couldn't overhear, she wrapped her arms around her middle and gave into the deep belly laughs she'd had to keep inside for fear of hurting his feelings. He was a man, after all, and the male ego did need to be stroked and respected at times.

Dear heavens, I might fall for him if I'm not careful. As it was, she wasn't sure in what capacity she wanted him, but she knew one thing for certain—she did want him.

Chapter Five

Richard urged his horse down the lane that would eventually lead to Miranda Craythorne's home. Earlier in the morning, he'd woken from a particularly vivid dream about the woman. They'd been indulging in a rather scandalous bout of physical relations, in a shadowy corner of a ballroom no less. He'd come awake swearing he heard her low moans of pleasure. As a consequence, he'd realized he was alone with a swollen cock and no female around to alleviate its ache. Loath to bring himself to completion, he'd laid on his bed, stared at the cracked ceiling and thought of the myriad of cows all over the countryside until the urge faded.

That had been an hour ago and his thoughts hadn't calmed as easily as his cock. The possibility of coaxing Miranda into a *ménage* heated his blood; the possibility of having a woman care if he lived or died while on a mission warmed his heart. As of yet, neither had been secured. He tightened his grip on the leather reins. Riding staidly through the country lanes wasn't thrilling enough to match the anxious feeling building in his gut. He wanted to have domestic issues well in hand before he quit the country. Yesterday he'd had news of his next assignment; today was the time to live as if a demon chased him. A visit with misfortune's lady was in order, and if he was lucky, perhaps he'd find a use for the burgeoning erection that threatened to bedevil him again—as it did each time he even vaguely thought of the widow.

He guided the bay mare off the path. Then he bent low over her neck, let her have the lead and enjoyed the sensation of the early morning mist in his face as they flew across the countryside. Since he'd arrived home to England a week ago, the forced inactivity had gone to his head. When a man didn't have women, gaming, or physical activity to occupy him, he started thinking, and when that happened, sadness and self-pity usually followed. Richard wanted none of it. He refused to remember his past, but he'd be damned if he let his future dissolve the same way. Unfortunately, both were intricately related. He gritted his teeth. *I need a distraction.* He craved a challenge, the chance to outwit an opponent or at least do something to drain the restless feelings.

Miranda Craythorne would be just the antidote. If luck was with him, she'd be such for longer than a lonely morning in the drizzle. And, if not, well... he didn't want to think about that at the moment.

As he gained the top of a small hillock, he spied both Miranda and John riding back to the house from the opposite direction. Richard grunted. His friend had wasted no time with his courtship. A pang of jealousy stabbed his heart while he guided the mare down the slope at a gentle trot. John had always known what he wanted from life—Miranda. He'd even made a change of vocation in order to ensure the Runners didn't command his every moment. At times Richard wished he could be as sure, but being devastated once wasn't an emotion he wished to experience again. His saving grace was his position with the War Office. Nothing would change that. He lived for king and country now—not for the state of his own heart.

By the time he reached the stable yard, the misty drizzle had intensified. Neither his friend nor Miranda noticed his approach. He pulled on the reins and waited while John assisted the woman down from her horse. Her throaty laughter reached his ears and brought new life to his cock. Richard ignored his need as best he could. It was more important John find his stride with the lady. The poor bastard was besotted with Miranda. Hell, he'd been in love with the idea of her for as long as he and John had been friends. Honestly, he was due a bit of happiness, yet Richard couldn't help rolling his eyes when John, of course, didn't release Miranda once her feet were on the ground. The man was incapable of being aggressive in his affections, choosing instead the gentle approach. Richard snickered. *Wherein I prefer to show a woman exactly what I want and why.*

She attempted to duck out of his embrace, but John wouldn't be deterred. There was always something heartwarming about watching John romance a woman though. Like a dog with a bone, he didn't give up until he'd won the prize. Once John secured a quick kiss, he released her then happened to look in Richard's direction.

"How goes it?" John asked as Richard handed off his reins to a stable lad.

"Excellent, as always." He slid from his mount in time to catch a faint blush on Miranda's cheeks when she joined them. "I see the two of you are wasting no time solidifying your affections."

John glanced at Miranda and grinned. "I am increasingly carried away in her presence."

"So I saw." He flicked his gaze to Miranda, who whispered something into her mount's ear before allowing the stable lad to lead the animal away. He looked again at his friend. "I've had news by special courier last night."

"From the Home Office?" When Richard nodded John's expression sobered. Gone was the teasing suitor and instead, an intense air fell over him. "Shall I beg off this morning's entertainment? Miranda would understand. If you require a quick word—"

"No, no. It can keep until later." The last thing he wanted to do was ruin the progress John had made. His friend deserved the whole leg-shackled, brats-in-leading-strings life while Richard merely desired someone at home, thinking of him while he was far afield.

"Good morning, Richard." Miranda invaded their space. She touched his arm and kissed his cheek, putting an end to the conversation. "Would you like to join John and me for breakfast?" The persistent mist had dampened the feathers on her bonnet as well as her dress. The skirt showed the outline of her legs to perfection.

His cock twitched. He remembered how soft her skin had felt that afternoon in the curricle. If he could arrange it, he'd sample that skin again—and soon—but knowing she waited for an answer, he nodded. "That would be delightful."

"Excellent." Her blue-green eyes twinkled. A playful grin curved her rosy lips. "We'll visit a bit before having breakfast." She peered at John. "If you will both follow me, we'll adjourn to my conservatory."

John looked sharply at her. "Your conservatory? But how, and why now?"

"It's time. You earned the privilege from the peacock incident."

"Then you trust me?" The hope clinging to John's voice was disgusting.

"Yes."

"And Richard?"

Miranda glanced briefly at him. "I trust Richard because you trust him. It's time to advance our relationship, gentlemen." Her gaze lingered on Richard. "In all aspects. I welcome your courtship."

John nodded and a huge grin curved his lips. "Indeed."

Richard had no idea why the gist of the conversation was so important, but the pleased expression on John's face made him pause. Had the room been previously off-limits? With no option except to follow them both into the house, Richard stifled a sigh. At times he felt unwanted until he reminded himself he preferred things this way.

After a series of corridors, they entered a room that housed a wall of floor-to-ceilings windows, delicate lady-like furniture as well as gilded birdcages. Every inch of the room had Miranda's stamp. Did she spend her free time in this room with the birds? The sewing baskets and books on the tables indicated she did. He relaxed a fraction. Perhaps both he and John had passed an invisible hurdle though he had no idea how or why.

What exactly had occurred on that morning ride? Perhaps he'd ask John to enlighten him later.

He glanced at John, but his friend had wandered to one of the cages, seemingly absorbed in gaining the attention of a cockatoo, which turned his white-feathered back on John, having none of the friendly overtures. Richard stroked a fingertip along his thin mustache as he took a seat atop a brocade-covered cushion.

Miranda smiled at them each in turn. "I'm certain Eppson is still abed at this time of the morning, but Cook will be up. I'll bring in some tea and order a hearty breakfast for us all. Behave yourselves while I'm gone."

The second she left the room, Richard bounded to his feet. "The Home Office is sending me back to France."

"For what purpose?" John turned from his perusal from the bird. He clasped his hands behind his back. "Diplomatic relations between England and France, though chilly, aren't that bad for the moment."

"You're not far off the mark. Napoleon, as far as we know, is still ensconced in exile on St. Helena, but though the wars have been over for a good five years, the Home Office is worried about lingering sympathizers. They're concerned another incident will erupt, and after being spanked in both ground and sea battles in recent years, they want to stifle things while in infancy. Save face and all that." Richard shrugged. He could no more anticipate his orders or the whims of the Crown than he could ponder out what side of the cage the budgies would fly to. "I don't question things. I simply wish to be off."

John nodded. "Not that it would do any good if you did question it." The stare he gave Richard was hard. "When are you leaving?"

"By week's end."

"Gone how long?"

"A few months, but could possibly be home for Christmas. After that, I've heard talk they want to send me with a contingent to South Africa." He rubbed a hand along his stubble-covered jaw. He'd been so anxious to get outside earlier he'd left his rooms without shaving. Did Miranda care he looked less than put-together? "There is one last thing."

"Yes?" John cocked an eyebrow.

"I'd like to solidify a direction in Miranda's affections before I leave." He edged away from the budgie cage. Something about the frenetic activity of the avian occupants made him nervous. "I'd rather not quit the country without knowing what I have to come home to—or not." He'd had enough of returning to empty rooms in London, and there was only so much solace he could seek in the perfumed arms of the demi-monde before it grew distasteful.

I need more, just not enough to stifle—enough to make what I'm doing seem worthwhile.

"Understandable." John rocked back and forth on his heels. "I've made some headway, but you should conduct your own campaign to win her from your perspective. I cannot do everything, you know."

Richard narrowed his eyes. "Obviously. You and I have much different styles." His mind jumped to how silky and plush Miranda's lips had felt against his and how sweet she'd tasted during their kiss. He swallowed a groan. "In fact, the more she tempts, the better likelihood I'll bend her over the handiest piece of furniture and have my way with her."

John chuckled. "Been a long time, has it? I thought you had little trouble in the female arena."

"I don't." Richard put distance between them. His stomach clenched from the good-natured teasing. He'd always been confident about women and using them for his own sexual need. The situation with Miranda felt different. "There haven't been any who interested me as of late. Besides, I rather think you've spoiled me with talk of your lady fair."

"Ours, remember." He flicked his gaze toward the door as Miranda came into the room carrying a silver tray full of tea things. "I haven't spoken of the arrangement to her recently, but I think she'd be willing to listen." He lowered his voice. "Besides, you can be persuasive when you want, as well as charming. And she enjoys being kissed."

"By you. Don't be a dolt, John. This situation would perplex even a woman used to the idea." His chest tightened when Miranda looked his way with an inviting smile. Yet he knew an insane desire to try. "I'll see what I can do." He strode across the room, closed the door and then turned the key in the lock.

Why did it feel as if he was about to embark upon the most dangerous mission of his life?

Though the misting rain had chilled him, John declined a cup of tea. He'd let Richard have all of Miranda's attention for the moment. It was crucial that Richard manage to captivate Miranda's affection, for only God knew if he'd return from his assignments away. John cast a glance to the two of them. They both sat on a settee, talking quietly of banal topics such as the turn in the weather and juicy tidbits of gossip regarding the area's gentry.

John grinned and moved to regard the birdcages once more. Richard had enough town bronze and intelligence to interest a curious woman like Miranda, and she possessed enough feminine wiles and gumption to keep the man on his toes. In another time, perhaps, they might have made a match of it. John's stomach pitched even as his heart squeezed. It was more than obvious the two of them would suit. And what if they did? What would he—John—do about it? After all this time, would he lose her to yet another friend? John stifled an annoyed sigh. *Stay the course.* As the temporary panic subsided, John's confidence in winning Miranda returned. Richard wasn't looking for a permanent arrangement. John, more than any of Richard's other contemporaries, knew the high cost of Richard's private life and why he refused to let relations with a woman go past a light affair. The threesome would hold.

He tapped a fingertip against the budgie cage. In a flurry of wings, the flock of colorful birds flew to the opposite side of the enclosure. They eyed him while their little chests heaved from excitement or fear. John smiled and edged around the cage to the side they clung to. Again, the birds lit out across the cage, only this time, a few remained to watch him with heads cocked as if wondering who he was and why he bothered with them.

In a way the birds were much like Miranda. Winning them required nothing more than charm and patience. He touched one of the birds' clawed feet with a fingertip. He felt its rough texture before that bird, too, joined the others. Well, he had more than enough time. He'd wait them all out.

Through the golden bars of the cage, he watched his friend and Miranda interact. Richard had abandoned his tea in favor of moving close to her on the settee. He'd snaked one arm along the back of the furniture while he stroked Miranda's cheek with the other. John stifled a snort of laughter. Typical opening overture from Richard. He thought if a woman let down her guard enough for him to touch her cheek, the rest of the seduction would be easy. John searched Miranda's face for a reaction. A faint hint of a blush stained her skin. No doubt Richard had whispered something risqué to her. And the hand holding her teacup shook. Amber liquid sloshed perilously close to the rim. Ah, it would seem Richard enjoyed success.

John moved to the cage holding the cockatoo. He silently wished his friend luck. *Poor bastard.* Five years ago, Richard had been desperately in love with a woman, enough to offer for her. During their engagement, Richard had made an enemy of a band of rabid Napoleon-sympathizers. While he'd been away in France, a few of the men snuck into the home of Richard's fiancée and murdered her and her family in cold blood as retaliation for Richard's part in putting down the heart of their rebellion. Of course, the men had been brought to justice, but when Richard returned to England, he was a changed man.

Richard had vowed never to become so involved with a female that he'd give his heart again. Because he loved being a spy for England, he had no intentions of quitting and now, his motivation was renewed tenfold. He'd taken his fiancée's death harder than anything else in his life, which was why John had offered him the chance to be a third in the few relationships he'd conducted. Yes, he'd felt sorry for Richard, but was still hopeful his friend would find peace in the life he'd chosen.

Giving him a bit of solace in a *ménage a trois* seemed right. Richard didn't need to commit or lose his heart but could still feel that someone cared about him.

A soft, feminine sigh broke into his musings. John looked past the cockatoo toward the settee in time to see both Richard and Miranda slip into a reclining position while locked in a kiss that would grow heated if Richard played his cards right. John couldn't help his grin. He silently wished his friend well then turned his attention to the cockatoo. The big, white bird stared back at him with unblinking black eyes. Its black talons grasped a branch inside his cage.

"I wonder what secrets you know?" he said to the bird.

The cockatoo edged closer on its perch. It cocked its head, the curved black beak menacing in the soft light of a nearby oil lamp. It bobbed its head a few times before lifting up a foot and gnawing on a talon.

John shivered. He shoved away his distaste. If he wanted to win Miranda, he needed to make friends with her feathered companions. "My name is John."

The crest on the bird's head went up in all its yellow-and-white glory. The bird put down its foot and bobbed its head. "Miss John." It clucked after that but said nothing else.

"Ah, no. You're mistaken. I'm a man. *Mister* John." Though he felt silly conversing with—or rather to—a bird, he couldn't help it.

"Miss John." Again the cockatoo bobbed its head. "John will come."

"Oh." John stared at the bird. The bird stared back but kept quiet. Eventually, its crest lowered, and it regarded him with cold eyes. "Oh!" The avian captive hadn't made a gender error.

It must be repeating something Miranda had told it—multiple times. It was highly unlikely the bird learned those words only from hearing them once.

Had she hoped he would come for her? How often did she talk to her birds about him?

Warmth spread through his chest. She'd thought of him, and recently too. Had she wanted him since that kiss they'd shared at the house party? He glanced at the cockatoo, but it had settled on the far side of the cage with its beak tucked beneath one wing, clearly done with the conversation.

I knew my instincts weren't wrong.

He walked around the bird cages and approached the settee. Miranda lay on her back with her skirts bunched around her waist. One leg was bent at the knee and the other had fallen off the furniture giving his friend full, unimpeded access to her nether bits. Richard had a hand between her pale thighs. He glided his fingers along her folds. Was she wet already from Richard's attention? Would she encourage him to join the intimate scene? John's cock pressed with urgency against his riding breeches. He rubbed a hand along its length and groaned in slight relief before continuing his perusal.

Her bodice had been shoved down and her breasts exposed. Her pink, pebbled nipples pointed upward. A flush mottled the creamy skin of her chest—a good indication of her arousal and the perfect picture of a woman gripped in full desire.

Damnation, she's beautiful.

She arched her back as Richard rolled one of the erect buds. A throaty moan escaped her. His pulse quickened and his cock went harder still. He couldn't wait to touch her breasts himself.

When Richard glanced up, John grinned. Of course it had been Richard who'd coaxed her into such a state of undress, not to mention putting her on the precarious edge of coming undone. He wouldn't have been happy stopping with a mere kiss, but that didn't mean John couldn't join in.

No matter how much he wanted Richard to belong and feel part of a greater whole, a fierce wave of possessiveness slammed into him. Miranda was his woman too. Her needs and concerns were his first priority. The urge to make certain she was satisfied grew strong.

John came around the settee and gazed down at her. "Is this a private tryst or would you prefer additional stimulation?"

Her eyes popped open, dark with desire, and she met his gaze. A brilliant smile parted her lips. "Obviously it's not private as we're skirting the bounds of propriety already." She struggled into a sitting position and thwarted Richard's fondling in the process. "Any stimulation is welcome. However," Miranda slid a wistful glance to Richard. "we've gotten carried away by the moment and should probably stop in the event..."

"Oh, no." Richard's grin bordered on wolfish. He relocated to the floor at her feet. "John, if you please, put our lovely widow onto your lap."

Miranda sighed while John took a seat. "But, we shouldn't. What you and I just shared is enough until—" She squealed when John hauled her onto his lap and arranged her so she reverse-straddled him, with her back to his front.

"It's never enough," Richard rejoined.

John chuckled. He'd heard Richard use this argument before. She wouldn't win. John pressed his nose into her hair and inhaled her floral scent. Her trembling transferred to him, and he smiled. She was excited and needed the release. "You are well and truly caught, my dear." He nodded at his friend. John spread his legs which naturally opened hers and allowed Richard to feast upon her folds. "He won't stop until he's made you fly. Best give in and let him have his way."

"He's correct." Richard spread her legs even wider. He winked. "What kind of a gentleman would I be if I didn't leave a lady with something to remember me by?" And then he ducked his head beneath her bunched skirts.

Miranda squirmed on John's lap. "Oh, oh..." She threaded her fingers through Richard's hair and held his head closer to her body.

"Relax and enjoy." John, not able to see what Richard did to her due to her skirting, cupped her bare breasts. Their warmth filled his palms. He squeezed the soft mounds of flesh and then brushed his fingers over her nipples. She moaned when he rolled them. Her head lolled backward, and she guided one of his hands tighter over the buds. Having her in his arms and experiencing each tremor and shudder that racked her body fired his own need. "I've dreamed of touching you, Miranda, of doing to you exactly what Richard is doing right now."

He didn't begrudge Richard the honor of tasting her most intimate of places. His turn would come. Instead, he licked at the sensitive skin behind her ear. He nipped a line of kisses along her neck. Beneath his tongue, her pulse fluttered wildly. With each pluck of her nipples, she writhed on his lap. Every movement she made sent sensation through his cock and balls.

He gritted his teeth and kept his focus on her in order to kill the desire to spend in his breeches. Richard kept her legs splayed. Moans and sighs escaped both Richard and Miranda as he continued his feast.

She bucked from Richard's ministrations. "Dear heavens, I'm... oh, yes... I'm..." A low keening cry drowned the rest of her disjointed statement.

John groaned from the sheer wonder of listening to her enjoyment. He continued to torment her nipples, and then putting his lips to the shell of her ear, he said, "Fall into it, love. Let me see you embrace the bliss."

With another soft cry, Miranda shattered in his arms. Her body stiffened. She arched her back. Seconds later she slumped against his chest. "Good heavens. I'd forgotten how wonderful that moment is."

"This is but one of the first you'll experience at our hands." He held her close and grinned while gentle shudders rocked her body. Richard came out from under her skirts, wiping at his wet face with the back of a hand. "What do you think?"

Richard cocked an eyebrow. Admiration gleamed in his desire-darkened eyes. "If Miranda is waiting for me when I come back to England, being away from home might not seem like such a chore at times." He forced a swallow. "If she's this responsive from just my mouth, imagine what she'll be like with my cock—our cocks—inside her."

"It's all I've thought of since arriving in Surrey." In fact, any more talk and his engorged member would explode. Maybe he should return to the bird cages until things settled.

Miranda stirred enough to readjust her bodice over her swollen breasts. "Gentlemen, you're correct. Relations with you both will be quite something. However, I have no strength to indulge you for the moment, and there will be breakfast soon besides."

Richard chuckled. He pulled her from John's lap and bundled her into his arms. "Thank you for the honor, madam."

John's chest tightened while the two of them embraced. It warmed his heart to know Richard approved of her. Hopefully, in the next few days, John would alleviate the remainder of Miranda's reservations as well as stake his own claim to her body, but did he want their relationship to stop at an affair?

Chapter Six

Miranda hummed a popular waltzing tune as she set out a collection of glass jars. A row of twelve sat to the side and sparkled in the mid-day light. Those contained a cheery, orange marmalade. Cook had bought a wonderful basket of the citrus fruit the day before and had been quite excited to transform it into the sweet preserves. They both enjoyed the snack on toast.

The still room was the other area of the house Miranda felt most comfortable in—second only to her conservatory. It was here she could work with her hands and make the berries from the brambles and the vegetables from her garden into something useful and tasty for the months to come. Today, she planned to put up countless jars of gooseberry and strawberry-rhubarb jam plus preserve tomatoes and a few pickled beets. No matter how friendly and relaxed she was with the staff, they all knew if she was in her stillroom, she generally didn't wish to be disturbed. Besides, she didn't mind helping Cook process the property's extra bounty. It really was a task large enough for several people.

While her hands were busy, she allowed her mind to wander. Many times she'd solved problems in her life working for hours with vegetables and herbs, sometimes until her pantries overflowed. At others, she'd pack big baskets with the extras and deliver them to her neighbors throughout the county.

Today was such a day when she needed to puzzle through the murky issues of her soul—namely how to continue allowing John and Richard into her house without inviting the local gentry to come after her with verbal pitchforks. Just thinking of the men brought a smile to her lips. As she stirred a huge pot of the strawberry jam, encouraging it to cool faster, she revisited the pleasurable session she'd experienced at Richard's hand—or mouth as it had been.

Hot moisture tickled the curls between her thighs from the memories of two days ago. Heat slithered through her belly as if his ministrations were even now occurring. It awoke a need for something much more satisfying. She remembered every lick and stroke from his tongue, every moment that clever muscle had penetrated her core in the quest for her completion. Her nipples tightened into aching buds. She swore she still felt John's hands on her breasts, kneading them while he'd encouraged her to give into the release.

Oh, and it had been glorious. Not even self-pleasuring could bring her to such bliss. She took a deep breath and let it ease out. Being with the men in such scandalous ways was an aberration, nothing more. It couldn't happen again, for if it did, scandal would surely call. Yet she couldn't help but imagine what having each man in her bed would be like. They kissed differently. It would stand to reason they'd make love differently as well. A shiver racked her body. The second she gave into physical relations, the mood between the three of them would change. Did she want it to? Wasn't she content being by herself on her estate with her birds?

Miranda dipped the tip of a teaspoon into the pink mixture and pulled it out. She blew on the contents then sampled the jam. Tangy sweet goodness exploded on her tongue. Perfect. Just like the two men who vied for attention and prominence in her life.

Stuff and nonsense. There is no such thing as a perfect man. She rolled her eyes and dropped the teaspoon to the counter, where it clattered against the scarred wooden length. *Why can I not stop thinking of them?*

After pulling several half-quart jars toward her, she ladled the rosy contents into the containers. She wasn't naïve enough to think that a quick turn in the sheets would solve anything, no matter how much her traitorous body might desire such an occurrence. Though she had known of John in the past, she knew next to nothing about Richard. It would take much more than daily visits for tea to have such an acquaintance. And while physical relations with a man were very nice and satisfying indeed, what she truly wanted was a man who'd pledge to take care of her while they grew into old age, a man who would support her in every endeavor she chose to undertake and a man who would protect her regardless of whether she was in the right of a matter or not.

Was John that man or was it perhaps Richard? Did it matter if she wanted them both?

She filled a few more jars as she attempted to figure out the conundrum. John might be as he'd already mentioned wanting to set up a nursery, but did she want that as well? For the mere fact she'd like to keep him safe from her curse, she certainly wouldn't accept a proposal from him. And Richard had already made it clear he wanted no part in a domestic sort of life, which meant any relationship with him would be strictly physical. Add John into the mix and she had the makings of a scandal broth even she couldn't squeak out of. For that matter, could she be happy with just an affair with the pair, without legally belonging to either of them? She'd enjoyed being married, of taking a gentleman's name and of being introduced to his peers as his wife, yet look how all three unions had ended.

I'm not strong enough to endure more of the same.

A long sigh escaped her as she fitted the lids to the jars and worked the clamps. She did so enjoy having a man about the place dancing attendance upon her. It made her feel more alive than she had in years. Why did she need to choose between a life of pleasure steeped in scandal or a recognized union which would leave one of the men out in the cold? She wanted to do what she pleased and not worry about the potential backlash each man might receive. Neither deserved to have their careers damaged for a bit of fun between the sheets. Plus, how much of herself would she lose in the process and how much of her freedom?

She twirled a strand of hair around her finger. *What a muddle I've fallen into.*

Eppson cleared his throat, effectively interrupting her musings. "I beg your pardon, Mrs. Craythorne, but that annoying gentleman, Mr. Goddard, is back. He's demanding that he see you, says he refuses to be dumped in the parlor yet again."

"I'll wager he doesn't relish it." His patience had been sorely tested already this week, but if he truly wanted to win her regard, he'd persevere. She couldn't help the quick smile that jumped to her lips. It would seem John was as noble and true as he'd said. Miranda glanced over a shoulder at her butler. "Thank you, Eppson. He's not annoying. He *is* determined though. As he should be." Heaven help her, she truly enjoyed the attention he showered upon her. "Where is he at the moment?" Her heart fluttered to know he was near.

"In the back parlor. Apparently, he'd been wandering about the lawn with the peacocks before he finally came to the house."

Poor John. "I'm quite busy. Please show him here."

The butler harrumphed. "Be mindful of cads and liars. They'll do you no good."

She turned her attention to her canning once more. "Thank you for the warning, Eppson. Mr. Goddard is neither of those things. Now, bring him here. And please, unless the King himself pays a visit, I don't wish to be disturbed again." Though she was fond of her butler, and he'd been with her through every bad thing in her life, at times, his concern was smothering.

While waiting for John, Miranda put another pot on the wood stove and mixed the ingredients for the pickling liquid. The sharp scent of vinegar wafted to her nose, eased slightly by the aromatic spices of bay and juniper berries. As she added a measure of sugar to the mix, the click of the door closing caught her attention. "John, is that you?"

"Who else would it be, my dear?" The unmistakable rattle of the key in the lock then the tumble of the mechanism followed his question. "Are you expecting another gentleman?"

"Not tonight... unless you've brought Richard with you?" She moved the pot from the heat to let the contents cool before use.

"Richard is out of pocket for the moment. He rode to London yesterday to conduct last-minute business that couldn't wait until his next time on English soil."

"Oh. He is leaving again soon?" A knot tightened in her stomach. Though she understood he enjoyed his livelihood, she hated to think of him in danger. Away from her, spying for king and country, she couldn't bring him comfort if he needed it.

"Yes, in a few days. He won't return until the holidays."

"Poor Richard." Her heart hurt for Richard's chaotic schedule. "He must lead a lonely life. I can't imagine being away from home all the time, but I don't begrudge him the travel. I quite enjoyed it when I did it, but I had traveling companions in my husbands."

John came around the counter and sat upon the stool on the opposite side. "He prefers his life *sans* attachments." His eyes reflected shadows, but he didn't share his knowledge. "In his defense, he has good reason, and no, I won't tell you. It's his history. You'll need to charm it out of him."

"I thought it was the two of you who needed to charm me?" She started peeling the skins from roasted beets.

"And so we are, though your schedule isn't making the endeavor easy. Where have you been for the last two days? I certainly hope you haven't been avoiding me." He stuck a finger into one of the jars and sucked the rose-colored treat from his skin.

Heat rushed through Miranda's body. Saliva filled her mouth at the thought of licking the remainder of the jam from his finger. She swallowed. The paring knife cut deeply into one of the beets, nearly severing the vegetable in half. "Yesterday

I met with two potential clients who might use my matchmaking services. The day before I visited with a friend who lives some miles away. My friend's friend is... well, her family says she's touched in the head."

"You don't believe that assessment?" John commandeered a teaspoon and tucked into the jam with enough gusto she'd thought he'd never tasted the sweet treat before.

"Not exactly." She continued to peel beets, mostly so she wouldn't have to stare into his eyes and fall deeper into those enticing depths or beg him to spread the jam onto various places on her body so he could lick it from her skin. "I think Miss Bennett is a perfectly lovely woman though misunderstood even if she is nearing the age of being on the shelf. I believe she harbors passions that have been unmet as yet."

"Will you match her then?" He trailed his tongue along the bowl of the spoon. "If you say she's of sound mind, I'm sure there's a gentleman somewhere who will agree."

"I'll wait and see what happens before I interfere." Now that the peeling had been completed, Miranda sliced the beets into half-inch rounds. "I'm told there will be a new neighbor moving in. Perhaps he's a bachelor on the prowl."

"Ah. Already you have plans for the girl. You can't help it."

"I want everyone to find happiness in the arms of someone." She smiled. "It's one of the best feelings in the world."

"Such a romantic." He pinned her with a glance that brimmed with wicked mischief. "Where is your cook? Wouldn't she take care of all of this?" He gestured with the spoon to include the workspace.

"Cook has the day off to visit her brother and his family in the neighboring village. She'll stop at the market on her way back, but yes, she and I accomplish the canning together. It's quite therapeutic if my mind is in a tither."

John again looked down the worktable. "It would appear you've been lost in thought for some time."

"Perhaps." Let him think what he wanted. It would be good to keep him guessing.

"And Eppson? Will he pop in on us from a secret passage?"

What was the man about? "Since I don't have one of those, I'd say no. Besides, he knows better than to interrupt me while I'm working in here. I've already warned him once today, specifically since I learned of your arrival." She stopped slicing, mindful that the vegetables had stained her fingertips pink. "For the moment you have me all to yourself."

"Then I suppose I should make the best of that moment, hmm?"

A shiver coursed down her spine. "Yes, and you can do that by handing me the tray of jars behind you please." He'd need to work a little harder if he wanted her undivided attention.

"Vixen." He hopped off the stool but brought the tray to her counter and slid it toward her. "You always did know how to encourage men to do your bidding."

Miranda smiled. She cocked an eyebrow. "No. If I recall, giving a man a smile or kind word then asking him to do a favor isn't classified as 'bidding.' It's more like helping out. If a man can follow simple instructions without arguing or confusion, he has great potential to pass the next hurdle." She gently placed the beet rounds into the jars. Four glass containers were left over, which meant she'd need to return to peeling and slicing.

"What's that next challenge, Miranda?" His question was low and filled with unidentified emotion.

She shrugged. Why should she play coy now? She knew John wished a courtship. Perhaps it was time to see what he had to offer, and she had said all three of them needed to advance their affair. "Allowing me to form an attachment."

His grin widened. "Ah, it seems I'm slowly insinuating my way past your defenses. Give me another few days and I'll be tugging on your heartstrings."

Flutters tickled her stomach. Flirting had always been one of her favorite parts of courtship. "Eppson told me you visited with the peacocks before you came in."

"I was, actually. The birds only attempted to rush at me once today. I suppose they recognized me from the other day—or else they figured I'm no threat and not worth their time." He ate another spoonful of jam then laid the spoon on the counter. "I learned something very interesting in that quarter."

"Oh?" Why had he been out in the yard to begin with? "I thought you hated my birds."

"That assessment was made in haste." He rapped his knuckles on the workspace. "I didn't understand them on the first day. Now that I've spent quality time with them and let them nearly peck me to death, I've made a discovery... or a correlation if you will."

"Yes?" She finished peeling the remainder of the beets.

"The muster is much like Society. They've made themselves into something all the other peacocks and hens desperately want to be a part of, yet the muster itself is very restrictive and a bit snobbish. Which leaves the outsider no choice except to formulate a plan."

Miranda uttered an unladylike snort. "You believe one of my peacocks devised a plan to join the muster?"

"Oh yes." John came around the counter and sidled close. "John the peacock has affectively played his hand—or foot as the case is—well. He's pretended he doesn't care if the renegade female notices him because he knows she wants a place in the muster more."

"Meaning? Will she use him for an invitation?" She couldn't concentrate on slicing the remaining beets while John's body heat seeped into her back as he moved directly behind her.

"Meaning he wants her. He doesn't care what the muster thinks, so he's bided his time and courted the single peahen." John placed his hands on her shoulders and smoothed his palms along her arms. "He's been patient. He's been respectful of her skittish ways. He's pretended he wasn't interested in her at all, which made him all the more appealing to the wary female." He traced his fingertips along her nape and then down her back. "Finally, his persistence has paid off."

Tremors danced along her skin, from his touch or his words she couldn't say. "Whose?" Miranda couldn't ascertain what he talked about, not when his fingers on her body infused her with such heat she feared she'd melt into a puddle at his feet.

"John's, of course." He placed a whisper-soft kiss on her nape. "The peacock, to clarify. As I walked the lawn, the peahen approached that fine, white fellow without malice. John accepted her overture with grace and warmth." His breath steamed her skin. "He treated our reluctant, independent peahen to the full splendor of his tail plumage."

His use of "our" sent a tremor through her heart. "Are they getting along then?" Her heartbeat accelerated. She loved being so close to him and adored it even more that he'd taken an interest in something as important to her as the birds.

"Oh, famously, but only time will tell." He moved closer. "Just prior to my gaining access to the house, both he and the peahen retired into the underbrush. I, for one, am hoping for a clutch of eggs." The hard bulge of his engorged cock rubbed at the small of her back.

"Why?" When he played his fingers up and down her ribcage, her breathing shallowed. Shivers followed in his wake and excited each nerve ending.

"Why not? You wish for more peacocks, especially with this couple." Through her dress and the muslin apron she wore on top, John cupped her breasts. His large hands engulfed them, his heat branding her, while frissons of sensation flowed through her body. "Why shouldn't I hope that for you?" He truly sounded excited about the peacocks, and then he pressed a kiss to the side of her neck and her thoughts scrambled.

"What a nice gesture. Thank you."

Good Lord, Miranda, could you be more addle-pated with a response?

Warmth flooded her chest. Perhaps he wouldn't be buried in his work as he had been when she'd seen him at that long ago party. If relations between them progressed, would he be content to live in Surrey? She frowned, undeterred by John's caressing. "I'm taken aback that you spent time observing them." Miranda stilled her fingers. She laid her knife on the board. It wouldn't do to keep hold of it while John's hands burned through her clothing. If she turned around, he might release her, plus she'd get beet juice on his clothes and stain them.

"I've mentioned before that I've changed. I've grown from the man you met all those years ago, Miranda." He increased the play at her breasts, kneading, stroking, massaging. "For you, I plan to do much more."

"Is that right?" Her knees threatened to buckle as he brushed his thumbs over her nipples. They hardened from his teasing. Her breasts ached and grew heavy, even more so the longer he fondled. Though she stifled a moan, she wanted his touch, skin-to-skin. "I'm happy to hear it." Molten heat wound through her belly and lower into her core.

"I'll do whatever you need me to do in order to win you this time. Soon, I plan to befriend the budgies." He trailed a line of kisses along her jaw and ended at her ear, and all the while he rolled her nipples. "I've already made the cockatoo's acquaintance. That bird told me a couple of interesting tidbits."

"Such as?" Why did he want to talk about birds at the moment when he could use his mouth for kissing?

"Our feathered friend said you missed me and that you wished I'd come." John nibbled on her earlobe. "I'm glad. It puts me in a very interesting position."

Miranda sighed. She couldn't help it. Locked in such an intimate embrace made her feel cherished, but would he come up to scratch and pledge his protection? Could she leave their relationship at only that or did she want more? Realizing he waited for an answer, she said, "How so?"

Gently, as if she were made of delicate china, John turned her around, so she faced him. His eyes had darkened and matched his intense expression. "To find out if what the bird said is true." He traced her lower lip with a fingertip. A shiver shot down her spine. "Have you missed me? Did memories of the kiss we shared at that house party where you met Oliver keep you warm when your bed was cold and empty? Have you wanted me for as long as I have you?"

She swallowed around the lump in her throat. "I've thought about you over the years, yes, I won't lie." She took a shuddering breath and let it ease out between her lips. If she continued to hold his gaze, she might drown in those blue depths and forget about everything else. To occupy her hands lest she pull on his shoulders and ravish his mouth, she wiped them on her apron. "Even though I was happy with Oliver, as well as Theodore after him, I never could forget that one moment with you, that wonderful second when I gave you everything and thought we would—"

"Indulge in a harmless dalliance that might have led to other things—things which would leave both of us quite satisfied for that moment and even beyond?" His eyes were bright points of light, roiling with emotion she refused to identify for fear she'd be wrong.

"Yes. But I'm not the woman I was all those years ago. I was careless and hasty back then. I thought I couldn't live without a man in my life, and would have thought nothing of meeting a gentleman in a shadowy corner for the sheer thrill of it, even more so if there would be a hint of marriage at the end."

"And now?"

"Now, I rather enjoy my independence, yet..." She swept her hungry gaze along the sturdy breadth of his shoulders and the broad expanse of his chest. Oh, how she'd longed for this very moment. "I don't know how harmless it would have been, as I'm quite sure I couldn't have refused you."

Barely had the words left her mouth before John swept her into his arms with a little growl. He trapped her against the hard wall of his chest and the edge of her worktable. "Tell me you want me, Miranda. I need to hear you say it. No more hints and innuendos."

"I'm willing to give you a second chance." Her pulse rushed so hard through her veins she heard it in her ears. Unable to deny herself from touching him, she stroked a hand along his jaw. The faint prickle of stubble rasped against her skin. A muscle twitched beneath her fingertips. With every beat of her heart, she feared she'd shatter from need. For this one moment, she wished only to feel his lips and to have his body moving on hers. Worrying about scandal could wait; trying to puzzle out her future would benefit from a delay. In this one fleeting second, there was only her and him—the man who'd slipped through her fingers. "John, I want you."

He crushed his mouth to hers, claiming her lips with a strength she couldn't deny. One second she was conversing and the next all of her senses were consumed by him. The muscled length of him pressed into her softer body while the hard edge of the worktable cut into her hips. His arms around her felt like iron bands, his fingers fire as he played them up and down her spine. The warmth of his tongue as he tangled it against hers sent matching liquid warmth between her thighs. She moaned into his mouth and burrowed closer. His clean, crisp scent wafted into her nose and left his indelible stamp upon her brain.

This was her John, the man she'd dreamed of in the dark of her bedroom when she felt most alone. He'd been the one man she could never forget; the one man she'd always wished would come back into her life if for nothing else than to lay eyes on him one last time.

Except now, she wasn't ready or willing to give him up to fate or chance. Miranda threaded her fingers through the silky hair at his nape. She stood on tiptoe in order to feel the full extent of his kiss. Her hardened nipples rubbed against her shift, and she moaned. Would he touch her there and ease their ache?

He didn't, but he traced her back. Bit by bit he drew the hem of her dress up. Cool air circulated around her exposed legs. Seconds later, the heat of his hands seeped into her rear as he gripped her derriere. His fingers feathered over her skin, and she shifted in order to spread her legs, hoping he'd stroke her pulsing sex. Moisture coated her folds in anticipation of him playing there.

When he merely drew abstract patterns over her buttocks, she wrenched away to pepper his chin with kisses. "Perhaps we should retire—"

"No time." He grasped her hips and ground his pelvis into hers. "No doubt you can feel how urgent things have become."

"I can." Daring to be bold, she drew a hand between their bodies and caressed the impressive bulge of his cock where it pressed against his trousers. His breath hissed. She smiled and rubbed her hand along his length.

"I won't last if you keep on." He lifted her off her feet, unmindful of her squeal, and propelled her over the floor until her back connected with a wall. "What do the windows of this room look out upon?"

Miranda glanced over his shoulder. "Only the back gardens. There shouldn't be anyone there at this time of day." She didn't want to talk about the gardens or the grounds. "If you're concerned, we can move upstairs..."

"No, this will do quite well." John unbuttoned the front of his trousers and freed his cock. The engorged member stuck straight out, bobbing between them, rigid, dark-veined and waiting.

She wrapped a hand around his length. His hot girth filled her palm and jumped when she rubbed her thumb over its weeping tip. What would he feel like in her body or taste like on her tongue? "I cannot tell you how nice it is to be in a man's arms again."

Amusement warred with need in his blue eyes. "Not any nicer than me being in you." He dropped a kiss on her mouth. "I apologize that our first time has neither romance nor finesse behind it. More than likely it will be quick as well." He grabbed handfuls of her skirts and bunched them around her waist. "It's been rather a long wait."

She didn't protest when he urged one of her legs up to rest on his hip. The head of his cock rubbed along her wet folds as she opened to him. A host of shivers fell down her spine and clashed with the ones invading her insides. "I haven't been with a man since my last husband died." Her stomach clenched from nerves. No matter how much she desired John, or how much her body clambered to be joined with his, what if they weren't compatible...?

He shoved into her passage without warning, and then Miranda's world dissolved beneath a wave of pleasure. "Damnation, you feel so good." He pulled out only to thrust again. John groaned and held his position, fully sheathed. His breath stirred the loose hair at her temple.

There were no words she wanted to waste on how he made her feel. She grasped his shoulders and tilted her hips, wriggled them in order to take him in as far as she could. His thick, long length filled her, stretched her more than she'd ever been. Each tiny movement on his part set off a flutter of sensation through her core. Her insides tingled and tightened. She pulled him closer, wanting him to move yet hoping they could remain like this forever.

She'd never felt such a bond with anyone before. Another little piece of her heart left to become his.

John held her steady with his hands at her hips. His gaze softened and a mixture of awe and pleasure illuminated his expression. He closed his eyes and moved within her. Each penetration sent glorious sensations through her body.

With each slow, gentle thrust, Miranda lost yet more pieces of herself to him. He'd always been caring and considerate. Nothing had changed; she'd merely chosen not to see it in him for fear of being hurt. Now, in this one moment where her fantasies and real life collided, she discovered the reality was far better than her dreams.

Chapter Seven

John could hardly believe his luck. Miranda had not only responded to his advances, but she'd allowed him intimate access to her body. He slid his hands to her arse, holding her steady, while she clutched him closer with a leg around his hip.

"This is lovely." Her throaty statement burned through his blood like a wildfire. He wished he could hear her voice every day for the rest of his life.

He grunted, opening his eyes to hold her blue-green gaze. "I don't want our joining to be lovely." As it was, taking her with little pomp or circumstance was beyond the pale, but he couldn't help it. He'd wanted her, plain and simple. His rhythm increased as did his bid to claim her. Stronger. Harder. Faster. Each slide into her heat sent him closer to the edge. His balls tingled. "I want you to be so moved that you cannot consider a life without me." Though he'd made no secret of his intent with her, it felt right to reiterate it now.

"John, send my flying." Desperation filled her voice. Miranda dug her fingernails into his shoulders.

How could he deny her anything, let alone this? He pumped into her. Each thrust sent intense sensation racing along his cock until urgency usurped his need to prolong the act. Miranda's soft mewling sounds of encouragement increased in volume. She stiffened and shouted his name. She clawed at his shoulders and met his final drive. Her inner walls squeezed around him in a series of frantic flutters. His member shuddered and pulsed. His balls drew close to his body. John moaned and shoved deep through the contractions. Seconds later his cock twitched and emptied its seed.

As his ragged breathing and erratic heartbeat returned to normal, he let her leg slip from his hip. He backed slightly away. Sharing the intimacy with her had been every bit as wonderful as he'd hoped, yet the euphoria of the moment faded all too quickly. How could he be expected to go about his business without knowing he'd secured her hand? *Botheration. Why must such things be so complicated?* Miranda's skirts fell into place, but she swayed. He bundled her into his arms, content to merely hold her against his chest. Would the fact they'd shared a bout of impromptu sex change her mind regarding marriage, and if it didn't, could he be content not being with her on a permanent basis?

When she stirred, he kissed the top of her head and then released her. Miranda's smile rivaled the sun streaming in the windows. "You were correct. That was more than lovely." She cupped his cheek, her palm warm against his skin. "And better than I could imagine."

His chest tightened. "Fair warning, though. I don't plan for this to be our only carnal meeting." John claimed her lips in a gentle kiss. When he allowed her breath, he said, "Don't expect me to stay away. I'll be underfoot, as well as a nuisance, until you're mine. Longer than that, even." Would it be a matter of wearing her down by coming around often, or would she genuinely develop feelings for him?

Also, there was the matter of Richard.

He heaved a sigh, suddenly adrift with awkward confusion. "What shall we do now?" Not willing to let her know how conflicted his thoughts had become, he tucked his flaccid cock into his trousers then manipulated the buttons.

Miranda arranged loosened strands of hair back into the knot at the back of her head. "I'll finish the beets. If you fancy helping me, I won't turn you down."

"I had rather thought we'd talk about the future, but if this is all you're willing to give me for the moment, I'll take it." Despite the threads of disappointment twisting his gut, he resumed his seat on the stool.

"Don't fret, John. If I wasn't interested in the future, I'd have already asked you to leave."

Was that simply flirting, or did she truly mean it? Had she merely wanted him to service her? He shoved a hand through his hair. Never had he been so perplexed. "Very well."

A thrill of laughter escaped her throat. "Let me finish here. Then we'll talk in the conservatory. I do adore teasing you." She smiled. "For a big man, you certainly do resemble a little boy when you're disappointed or troubled."

Somewhat mollified and more than a tad embarrassed, John nodded. "Thank you." His Miranda had always been a bit of a minx, and she appeared to enjoy life regardless of her perceived misfortunes. It was one of the things he loved about her... but he wanted to love her for the rest of his life, and not from afar.

I can't rush it. I don't wish to spook her or else she'll refuse to see me. I won't lose her again.

"I'm holding a small get-together on Sunday night. Do you think you and Richard would care to come? I'd enjoy being with you both, together. The three of us need to talk."

"I'd like that." His blood heated. Was that her way of saying she wanted them in bed or did she merely want them for conversation? "I'll send a courier to Richard and let him know."

"That would be nice." No sooner had Miranda taken her knife in hand than a discreet knock sounded on the door. "Mrs. Craythorne, may I enter?"

She darted her gaze to his. "Eppson again." She touched a hand to her face. "Do I look presentable?"

"You're beautiful." John grinned. Wisps of her blonde-red hair clung around her forehead and nape while her cheeks blazed with healthy color. Anyone with half a brain would know she hadn't been merely spending time with her canning.

"You are a terrible liar, sir."

"Go find out what the old bird wants."

She crossed the room, unlocked the door, and yanked it open. "What can I assist you with, Eppson?"

"I apologize for interrupting you, ma'am, but your cousin, Miss Lythe, is in the parlor. She'd like a moment of your time if you're not already occupied." The butler's gaze strayed to John before he snapped it back to Miranda's face.

The remainder of their conversation was too low for John to discern. He narrowed his eyes. The cheek of the butler astounded him. Regardless of whether Miranda accepted a proposal from him, the need to relocate her to his townhouse in London grew strong. His servants knew their place and would never dream of dictating their opinions to their betters. No matter. His first priority was winning her heart.

He stood as Miranda approached. "Do you wish me to go?" Though he'd strived to keep the annoyance from his voice, he heard it and hated himself for it, but by God, the interruptions were not to be endured anymore.

"Absolutely not. If my cousin cannot make nice with someone I'm entertaining, she can either learn the art of tact or she can return later." Miranda's eyes twinkled. Her rosy lips curved with a smile. "Will you escort me to the parlor?" She untied the apron and removed it. By the time she'd tossed it onto a stool, he'd joined her.

"I will." He offered her his arm, bent at the elbow. "Lead on." When she laid her hand on his sleeve, warmth flowed through his limbs. This was what he'd wanted since the first day he'd seen her—Miranda at his side in a domestic setting. He remembered how divine she'd felt in his arms and around his cock, and his heart skipped. Oh, he meant what he said before. He'd claim her body again, but he wanted every bit of the woman she was. He'd loved her for too long to not see the dream into fruition. Their arrangement would work; he merely needed to apply more charm and insistence. Like John the peacock, he would prevail. His confidence restored, he patted her hand. "Let's see what your cousin has to say, shall we?"

As soon as he and Miranda entered the back parlor, the single occupant hopped to her feet and said, "Finally, Miranda. I thought you might still be abed at this hour."

John released Miranda's hand and moved to the far side of the room in order to observe both women. A blush jumped into Miranda's cheeks. Where the tall, thin blonde was in the current style, he much preferred Miranda's red-tinged locks and curvy figure.

"Oh, I wasn't abed, regardless of how hard I tried to go in that direction. I was otherwise occupied in my stillroom." She gestured to John. "Miss Annabelle Lythe, this is the Honorable John Goddard. He and I have been renewing our acquaintance over the course of the week."

"Pleased to meet you, Miss Lythe." John propped an elbow on the fireplace mantle and settled in. Was Miranda's blush due to embarrassment or pleasure? And how interesting his presence either way affected her so.

Miss Lythe simpered. She tucked a stray strand of blonde hair behind her ear. "Charmed, Mr. Goddard. I recognize your name as one of the men Miranda was excited to see at her party." The woman crossed the rug and extended her hand. "One of the men she wanted to match me with, but she made certain to place me within a different group instead once the night commenced."

"How very interesting." At no time during the party had Miranda introduced either he or Richard to this tall slip of a young lady. He relinquished his position at the mantle to take her hand and placed a light kiss on her middle knuckle. "I suppose she changed her mind."

"Perhaps." Miss Lythe's titter jarred his teeth. It was too shrill and smacked of desperation. "I'm glad you're here now, Mr. Goddard. Would you like to sit near me so we may talk?"

"No thank you. I'm rather comfortable here, where I can gaze upon both of you beauties." John nearly choked on his own laughter. While Annabelle blushed and sank onto a settee, madly fanning herself, Miranda narrowed her eyes and seemed ready to do him bodily harm.

Surely she couldn't be jealous over simple niceties?

Annabelle's lips pushed into a frown. "Pish-posh, Mr. Goddard. I was hoping to further our acquaintance as my cousin seemed in such a tither the other night when she feared you wouldn't show. It put ideas in my head, I can tell you." She peered at him, and her almond-shaped brown eyes sparkled. "Now I know why. You're quite dashing. Every woman's ideal. My cousin hinted you used to be a Bow Street Runner. How fascinating. Will you tell me about that?"

"Not today." A snort from Miranda distracted him from Annabelle's blatant flirting. "Thank you, Miss Lythe. I rather think you're right, but perhaps you should share with me all her glowing reports." If the girl was to be believed, it would appear Miranda had had every intention to match him with her that night. Why had Miranda changed her mind? Had it been Richard's appearance, or had that meeting on the terrace meant something more?

Miranda laid a hand on Annabelle's arm. "Stroking Mr. Goddard's ego isn't necessary." She encompassed them both with her gaze. "I simply came to the realization he wouldn't be the sort of man you'd need, my dear. He's rather intense for an untried girl."

John wasn't about to let her off that easily. "Ah, and what about me is so unappealing to such a vibrant young lady? Am I not pleasing?"

Miranda's blush deepened. "I merely meant you've established a certain life for yourself in London, while Annabelle wants a dozen children. That sort of domestic situation wouldn't align with your plans for the future. Think of your position, John."

"I have, which is why I dropped the Runners. Also, I'm not adverse to children. I want a couple, in fact." He held her gaze regardless that her cousin looked on. "This is all to the good, Miss Lythe. You see, no matter how hard you're looking to further my acquaintance, I'm afraid my regard already belongs to another. You may try, but I won't be moved."

The young lady's pout deepened. "Of course. This is always my luck. The good ones are already taken, and I'm left with the old and ugly fellows, or the ones with gout."

The girl was beyond gauche, though he had trouble stifling his laughter. "Do not lose hope, Miss Lythe. I'm sure the man for you is very close." He winked, as much to annoy Miranda as to flirt with Annabelle. "As for me, I need to secure the hand of the lady I'm interested in. That is proving more of a challenge since she's too skittish by half." He glanced at Miranda. She wouldn't look his way. He resisted the urge to hoot with laughter. "Despite my best efforts, it would seem she cannot give me her whole heart as she's under some ridiculous impression she's unlucky."

"Oh, my!" Annabelle gasped so deep she might have been attempting to deprive the room of air. "Miranda, I do believe Mr. Goddard is hinting he wants you." She darted a glance between John and Miranda. "He has that certain look, you know, the one that practically declares his intention before he ever says anything. How romantic. No wonder you refused to introduce us during your party."

"Is that right?" Miranda asked in a terse voice around what sounded like clenched teeth.

Miss Lythe giggled. "Now I understand what kept you so long on the terrace. You look much now as you did then, as if you'd engaged in particular exertions."

"Oh bother." The glance Miranda bestowed on her cousin brimmed with thunderclouds. "You have overstepped, Annabelle. This is none of your concern."

The blonde clapped her hands. Joy filled her expression. "Dear heavens, you fancy him in a romantic way too. How wonderful!" She grinned. "And you told me you didn't wish to marry again."

"I don't." Miranda clasped her hands so tightly in her lap the knuckles showed white. "I would advise you to abandon the subject. I do not wish to discuss such things with you right now."

John watched the interaction in breathless anticipation. Why was Miranda so flustered about the subject of marriage, children and him? Did she truly want those things with him, but fear held her back? As he opened his mouth to join the conversation, Annabelle spoke again.

"I cannot, Miranda, not now when there's a budding love story playing out before me." She fairly vibrated in her seat. "He's just what you need, cousin. Strong, handsome and with a pleasant demeanor and gainful employment so you needn't want for anything. Why wouldn't you give into his suit?"

Here was the opening he needed. Thank goodness for the annoying relative. "Yes, Miranda, I believe your cousin has laid things out quite splendidly for me. What do you require that I haven't offered as yet? Whatever it is, I shall endeavor to make it happen if that will hasten this courtship." What was more, his words were true. His heart constricted as he gazed at her.

If she wished him to visit a barber and have all his hair shaved off, then he'd do it if only to keep her for one more night. "All I have—all I am—is yours."

"I don't want you to keep chasing me." She sprang from her seat to pace the close confines of the room. "While I appreciate your regard and the fact you've wanted me for years, I cannot think while you're near. Your presence consumes me, John. You're too big, too overwhelming. I feel lost at times, and I need my independence. You must understand this. It's vital to who I am."

Whatever he'd thought she'd say in response to his teasing, that wasn't it. He left the mantle and took a few steps in her direction, but she shook her head and stopped him with an upraised hand. "Miranda, I beg your pardon. I had no idea..." Of what, that he went over the top with his attention? He had known it but couldn't control himself around her. "My goal has been merely to show you I can be all you need."

"While that may be so, I don't like being pressured or feeling trapped." The tendons in her neck worked with a hard swallow. "The more you chase, the more hunted I feel. That is no way to win me. Let me come to you on my own, like the peahen. I cannot be happy if you try and force it. Give me the space to make the decision."

"But you told me, in word and expressions, to try harder to win you. Have I not done that?" Truly, he was at odds. Hadn't he tried to follow her wishes? Why was she running scared now? Did the episode in the stillroom mean nothing after all?

"Excellent point." Annabelle nodded and the pheasant feathers on her bonnet wiggled madly. "I understand your conflict, cousin. If you and Mr. Goddard make a match of it, he'll demand you leave your home and everything you love in order to be with him in London. After all, that's the male mindset, isn't it, that they're the most important person in the pairing? What the woman wants means nothing once the marriage vows are taken."

"No, that's not what I would do." The conversation had gotten lost and was slipping away from him.

Miranda skewered him with a sharp glance that brimmed with hope. "Then you wouldn't want me to leave Surrey? Could you settle here?"

Once more Miss Lythe interrupted. "Oh, but that wouldn't work either, would it? This property isn't yours, Miranda. Doesn't your brother own it?"

"Yes, that is true." Miranda didn't take her gaze from John. "Even still, answer my question, John. Would you be willingly to live here in Surrey in order to win me?"

"I..." He cleared his throat. What a coil he'd been handed. "Well, obviously I'd want you to live in my townhome with me, as I do work in London. Surveillance would be rather difficult out of Town, but that doesn't mean—" Of course he wouldn't demand she sacrifice everything she loved. Perhaps she'd need to leave the birds behind, as he couldn't have the peacocks parading up and down the street, but he and she would work out a compromise.

"Oh, Miranda, don't do it." Annabelle jumped to her feet, her expression menacing. "He means to make you forfeit your independence in order to dance attendance on him."

"Annabelle, hush." Warning rang in Miranda's voice.

"No. Didn't you tell me a few days ago how much you loved your home? Has Mr. Goddard shared your fondness for this place or your menagerie? Does he love your birds as much as you do?"

"No, actually."

"Fustian! Haven't I put forth the effort with the peacocks?" This was beyond enough. Who was this chit to destroy everything he'd worked so hard to build with Miranda?

They both ignored his outburst. "Don't give in to him, cousin. You always followed your heart, and I idolized you for it. How can such a man own your heart if he doesn't share your interests?"

"I won't... that's not fair... we never discussed..." John drifted to a halt, lost in a morass of confusion and futility. What could he say to win what seemed like an impossible argument? "I didn't realize you wanted me to court your whole damn flock too."

Annabelle sniffed. She looked him over from head to foot. Her nose wrinkled as if he was smeared with peacock defecation then she gave Miranda her attention. "You've always done whatever your previous husbands wanted to do, followed *their* interests, be what you thought *they* wanted. Isn't it time to put yourself first for once?"

"I didn't mind doing such at the time..." Miranda's rejoinder drifted to a halt. "It didn't seem..."

"But it won't be like that." He glanced at Miranda and his heart skipped a beat. Cold shivers raced down his spine. Her face had paled. Her lips formed an O of surprise as if something her cousin had said held new meaning. Damnation, the blasted twit had made him out to be some sort of monster, two seconds away from wanting to lock her in a tower. "Miranda, please, I care too much for you to do anything that would make you unhappy. We'll talk about a life together. You know we can iron out the wrinkles."

Miranda shook her head. A wash of tears sparkled in her eyes. "Perhaps you should go for the time being. I need to think, to figure out what I want most from my life, and if you would fit into that. I cannot do that while you're so near."

"If you'll just listen to me and let me explain—"

"No." Her chin quivered. "We've shared quite enough for one day, thank you."

He rounded on Annabelle even though every instinct in him screamed to rein in his reaction, but his self-control, especially where Miranda was concerned, had never been strong. Would he lose Miranda for some untrue babble from an inexperienced female? Did she mean to discard him like rubbish now that her base needs had been satisfied? "Young woman, you should know your place next time, especially while interrupting conversations that don't concern you. This whole house is madness, from its guests, to the birds to the servants."

"See, Miranda? Now he shows you who he really is." Miss Lythe's grin was quite victorious.

At that moment John wanted nothing more than to throttle the girl. Instead, he ran a hand through his hair. "The affair between Miranda and I is not your business." His voice had risen into a semi-shout that brought Eppson to the door.

Annabelle gasped again. Her eyes widened. "You're conducting an affair with my cousin?"

Miranda's mouth opened and closed in an imitation of a trout, yet she didn't confirm or deny the statement. "There is a certain something there..." She twisted a curl around her finger, her face so pale he feared she'd succumb to a faint.

"Damnation, Miss Lythe, stop filling your cousin's head with stuff and nonsense you know nothing about." If he could speak with Miranda alone, he'd have a chance to fix the hideous problem that grew by leaps and bounds the longer the farce continued.

Both women gaped at him as if he'd grown two heads. Eppson drew himself up to his full height. He tugged on the bottom hem of his jacket. "Do you require assistance, Mrs. Craythorne?" He shot a glare in John's direction. One of his white-gloved hands curled into a fist.

"Yes, Eppson." Miranda turned toward her cousin. "Annabelle, will you please come above stairs with me. I'd like to lie down. This situation is too trying at the moment." She clutched one of her cousin's arms for support. "Eppson, will you escort Mr. Goddard to the door? I'm afraid I'm not feeling up to snuff at the moment, and when Cook returns, convey my apologies for leaving the stillroom in such a mess."

"I will, Mrs. Craythorne." Eppson waited until both women swept from the room before rounding on John. "If you'll come with me, sir. Your hat and gloves are in the hall. Also, I would advise you not to visit again unless Mrs. Craythorne personally invites you. She hasn't been this upset in a long time. You are not a good fit for her."

Inwardly, John seethed. A half hour ago, he couldn't have been happier. Now, due to a nosy relative and a cheeky servant, his prospects for matrimony—or even an illicit companionship—hung in tatters. Without recourse he followed the smug butler from the room, but spied the women as they mounted the stairs.

"Damn it, Miranda, this isn't over. Not by half. I will return, make no mistake. I won't give you up that easily." Then Eppson shoved his hat and gloves into his hands and all but thrust him in the direction of the front door.

Chapter Eight

Richard rapped at Miranda's front door with more force and annoyance than necessary. After he'd gotten John's message by courier late the night before, he'd subsequently left London and rode for Surrey, arriving back at the posting inn in the wee small hours of the night. Once he'd gained his rooms and cleaned off the worst of the travel dust and grime, he'd gone down to procure ale and food, but also found John attempting to drown his sorrows in a tankard, with two empty ones already on the table. It would seem the man had made a right good mess of his courtship of Miranda. Richard had listened, without humor, to a disjointed tale about a rushed coupling, a meddling butler, a troublesome miss, and the spooked widow, but the problem wasn't so large it couldn't be fixed—*I hope.*

Yet Richard forbade John from returning with him this morning. Not only was the damn fool well into his cups, he couldn't see what was right in front of his face where the widow was concerned. *I told him not to pester her. I begged him not to bother her every damn day, but did he listen? No.* He'd become even more of a bacon-brain. Plus, if his rambling account from the night before was to be believed, he'd been unable to curb his desire and had taken her in the stillroom without ever securing her hand or a promise.

What a coil we've landed in. Richard's mind fixated on the physical. The thought of John taking Miranda sent the blood rushing to his cock. Not only had John had relations with the woman, but he'd very nearly destroyed the chance for him—Richard. Well, he'd repair what his besotted friend broke, if only to enjoy his own chance with her. The recollection of her soft cries as he brought her to completion with his tongue swept through his brain. He swore he could still taste her slight tang on his lips. Devil take it, he wanted to know every inch of her body, wished to make an impression on her, be remembered fondly by her. Beyond that, he'd leave for assignment in two days. He needed his domestic situation settled before then. *Botheration.* This was why falling in love never paid off. Loving a woman meant a man's life—his thoughts—were no longer his own. *This is exactly why I refuse to go down that rabbit hole again.*

When no one answered his knock, he pounded harder. It was mid-morning. Someone in the house should be stirring even if it was only the servants. If they thought to deny him access, they could think again. No one denied him when he was determined to finish a thing. Finally, the door swung inward and the butler stood within the frame. The frown creasing his face pulled his whole expression downward as if it were on a string.

"I'm terribly sorry, but Mrs. Craythorne isn't receiving visitors today. If you'll leave a card, I'll see that she knows you called."

Chances were high if Richard left a card the butler would toss it into the rubbish bin. Miranda would never know he'd come by. "My mission here is of some import, Eppson. It's imperative I talk with Mrs. Craythorne at once."

The butler narrowed his eyes. "As I said, she doesn't want to see anyone, least of all friends of the man who upset her yesterday."

Richard caught the edge of the door before it fully closed. "Unless I hear the dictate from her lips, I'm not leaving." He forced the door wider and stepped into the foyer. "If you'd be so kind as to tell me her direction?" He would not be told to heel by some damn servant. "I'll be happy to go the distance myself."

Eppson harrumphed but wheeled around. "Follow me." Seconds later he showed Richard into the conservatory. "I beg your pardon, Mrs. Craythorne, but this gentleman refused to go away. He says he must speak with you urgently."

Miranda glanced over the rim of her teacup. Interest lit her blue-green eyes. She took a sip then set the cup on the table in front of her. The budgies' cheery twitter filled the air and lent the room a pleasant atmosphere in direct contrast to the tension crackling between her and Eppson. "Thank you." She rose but didn't smile. "Good morning, Richard." She smoothed the creases from the front of her plum-colored dress.

"Shall I wait here to escort him out?" The butler looked pointedly at Richard. "I did tell him you weren't receiving today."

"That won't be necessary, as I'm sure he won't stay long."

"But, madam—" The whine in the butler's voice set Richard's teeth on edge.

"I have no qualms about speaking with Mr. Howson. And Eppson, do *not* assume you know what's best for me. I didn't say I wouldn't see visitors." With her eyes narrowed, the red in her hair gleaming in the morning sunlight and her hands firmly planted on her hips, she was the picture of a vengeful goddess. "I said I wouldn't see *Mr. Goddard* today."

"Yes, ma'am." Eppson gave her a slight bow.

Richard's chest tightened to mirror the state of his prick. Good heavens, the woman was magnificent. He might not wish for romantic love in his life but he wouldn't discount capturing white-hot lust. He swallowed a groan. *I want Miranda too. John doesn't get to decide things for us both.* Certainly, his devotion wasn't to the extent of John's, but it didn't cancel his need. He couldn't wait to claim her and solidify his bid for her affections.

She nodded when Eppson lingered. "That will be all, then, Eppson. I have no other need of your services. Please don't disturb me while I'm visiting with Mr. Howson. I'm not best pleased with you at the moment."

"Very well, ma'am."

As soon as the butler departed, Miranda swept across the floor and closed the door behind him. She turned to Richard. "If you're here to plead John's case, you're wasting your time. I'm not pleased with him either."

"Actually, I'm quite perturbed with John at the moment." He paced the floor between the furniture grouping and the bird cages. Each time he came near, the budgies took flight and settled at the opposite side of their cage. "I won't apologize for his behavior. He is his own person. He makes his own mistakes. However, I'd urge caution where he's concerned. The last thing you need is to align yourself with a man who can't—or won't—support you in any endeavor you choose to make."

Miranda frowned. "I thought you were his friend?"

"I am." *And in my friendly opinion, the man needs a good thrashing to help him regain his common sense.*

"Wouldn't you try to put him back in my good graces or at the very least wish for his happiness?"

"I know him better than most, so probably not. He doesn't deserve a woman like you. And, at the moment, I care not a whit for his happiness. His mucking up doesn't deserve my good humor." Richard turned away to conceal a grin. Perhaps trying a different tactic with her would work better than pleading. In all his years of service to the Home Office, he'd found this particular way of dealing with stubborn people effective. "He's no good for you, Miranda. Best forget about him and let him stew in his own pudding."

"Perhaps he doesn't deserve that harsh of punishment." She was silent so long he thought she'd finished the conversation, and then she asked, "What of you?" Annoyance hung in her voice. "Do you wish to take his place? Has this been Providence's own gift?"

"Good God, no." Richard swung around. He removed his top hat and carefully laid it on a nearby chair. With slow movements, he took off his gloves and set them on his hat. "As I'm sure John has told you, I'm not interested in commitment or marriage. In fact, I leave for my next assignment in two days. There's always the possibility I won't return." He crossed his arms over his chest. "Yet now I'm forced to take time out of my leisure to make sure you won't take my nodcock friend back."

"What difference does it make to you?" Low-grade annoyance hung on her words.

You nearly have her. Go softly.

Richard tamped his reaction. "John's behavior doesn't merit your affection or even your love. He's too stubborn by half, and what sort of man loves a woman from afar for so many years without acting upon those feelings?" No matter that he'd been jealous of his friend's romantic affliction, Miranda didn't need to know that. "I thought he should've managed to declare himself as soon as your last husband died."

"Perhaps he wished to give me time to acclimate, to discover the woman I wanted to be *sans* marriage." She laid a hand on his arm. "He had his work. In the grand scheme, two years isn't that long."

His blood heated from the simple contact. "So you say." It took all his willpower not to react because one touch, one kiss, and his hard-won control would be all over. The matter would definitely not be settled if such an event occurred.

"It's not merely John's fault. I could have sent him a letter dropping a hint of my circumstances, but between mourning and the third marriage then mourning again..." She bit her bottom lip.

"What are you trying to tell me?" He would love to have more time to investigate how her thought processes worked. How conflicted she must be. As it was, there simply was no time. They would either all get on together or they wouldn't.

"It would appear I'm just as stubborn. I wanted him to come to me, to test the strength of his interest, but from all accounts, he'd been sowing his oats far too well."

He couldn't stand silent and let her think the worst of John even though his goal was to make her see her own error. "John was only with other women during the times you were married, sweeting."

"Oh?" There was no mistaking the hope in that one little word.

"Absolutely. In fact, just when the poor bastard screwed his courage to the sticking point to approach you after Oliver's death, you'd remarried in a twinkling. John was devastated. It took me three weeks to talk him down from the boughs and another two to get him out of the local tavern." Let her stew on that for a while.

"I had no idea." A waver moved through her voice. "I suppose years of stupidity are hard to conquer—on both our sides."

"Yet you had a tiff with him yesterday. That doesn't bode well for the future."

Miranda sighed. Her animosity fled under a mask of worry. "I allowed emotions to carry me away instead of speaking about my concerns to him, but I fear he'll smother me with good intentions."

"He might." Richard let down his guard enough to take her hand and stroke his fingers up the inside of her arm. Goose flesh followed in his wake. She wasn't as indifferent as she wanted him to think. "You are attracted to him."

A shiver racked her body. "I am. I wonder if it's enough. I'm tired of putting my dreams to the back of my mind for those of a husband's. Do I not matter?"

"You do, which is why I urge caution where John is concerned; otherwise, his passions will consume you in his desire to possess and protect you." He smoothed his palm over her shoulder then followed the curve of her neckline with a fingertip. "I could help, except we're all at an impasse, aren't we?"

"Are we?"

"After the debacle with John, I should say so."

A shuddering sigh escaped her throat. She pressed closer to him until their bodies almost touched. "I was under the impression you wanted to be part of a *ménage* relationship. Have you changed your mind?"

"I have not." Richard traced a path along her collarbone then moved upward to stroke the creamy skin of her neck. His cock thickened and flirted with the front of his pants for no other reason than he touched her and was near enough to smell her faint floral scent. "It matters not what I wish for if you'll reject John. He is key to the arrangement, and I refuse to be in the middle of your disagreement. That would be torture indeed."

"But, he must understand I am *not* an object to be possessed."

"I'm sure that he does. He is merely impatient." He cupped her cheek and grinned at her tiny hitch of breath. "I'd be quite content to play mediator in your relationship. Think of me as a buffer or protector. I can make certain John tempers his overbearing ways while securing the freedom you crave. The moment you feel too tied to hearth and home, you only need to tell me. I shall whisk you off to a far corner of the world and flood you with pleasure until your good mood returns. That is the glory of being me."

Her breathing increased slightly. "Being irresponsible?"

"Oh, wickedly so and quite unapologetic about it." He drew the pad of his thumb along her bottom lip. "The choice is yours, but above everything, I want you to feel comfortable and happy with both of us."

I've almost got her. Women such as Miranda needed to feel in control but didn't wish to hurt anyone's feelings making decisions or be seen as cold or uncaring. He'd gladly take away her angst in order to mend the relationship and give them all a chance.

She met his gaze. Hers roiled with unnamed emotion. "I'll admit I'm curious how a threesome would work, but what of you, Richard? How can you think your heart won't be engaged?"

"I won't allow it." It was his turn to mentally retreat. He took a step backward. "I refuse to open myself up for hurt again."

"Don't think you can manipulate me without some sort of retribution falling on you." She chased him until the settee blocked his flight. "Why are you so skittish?"

"It's not for you to know."

"Hmm." Her eyes twinkled in the morning light. "I may not be able to manage my own romances, but I can see other peoples' amorous problems. You were in love once, weren't you?"

Caught between her curiosity and the settee, he fought with his reticence to share and his desire to let her see why he wouldn't commit to a specific future with her. He forced down a hard swallow. "Yes." He'd only told his story to John, who took it at face value and didn't ask questions. With Miranda, it would be different. Would she force him to relive the pain or make him analyze why?

She pushed her body into his and encouraged his arms around her with all the skill of a seasoned courtesan. "Tell me. I want to know what made you into the man you are."

"So you can change me?" He'd never admit how good she felt in his embrace or how the insistent pulse of his cock reminded him he was still alive and vital—needed.

"No, so I can hold you and include you, to tell you that you're still worthy of love even though things went desperately wrong the last time."

His chest tightened. His heart ached from her easy acceptance, but he shook his head. "That may be, except I cannot open my heart or soul to such hurt again. I've made a habit of being shallow and of indulging only in the physical. If that makes me a cad or a scoundrel, so be it, but that won't change. It can't."

"I respect your stance." Miranda slid her palms up his chest then locked her hands behind his neck. "Tell me what happened. Were you married?"

Bugger. The woman was good. "Engaged. Several years ago. While I was on a mission for the Crown, an unsavory man in the Home Office revealed my identity to a few of Napoleon's supporters." A wave of familiar sadness welled inside of him. "Not only did they betray England, they tracked down the woman who was most precious to me and killed her in cold blood one morning, along with a few of her family members."

"Why?"

"They could, and they were making a statement that England was being too complacent. The fact she was a French expatriate didn't help matters." He tamped the urge to lash out. After all these years, the whole incident still hurt. He buried the pain deep inside. It was his alone to bear. No one could take it from him, and he didn't deserve to give it up. He must always remember.

"I'm sorry."

He nodded, appreciating her simple words. "The murderers were brought to justice before I could return to England. By then my fiancée had already been buried and everyone had had a chance to make peace with her death." Richard attempted to pull out of Miranda's embrace, but she held him fast. He relaxed slightly, glad for the support. "Her parents cited me and my dangerous occupation. I couldn't fault them, as I'd blamed my livelihood too. Still do."

"Yet you didn't give it up."

"I couldn't. Perhaps I loved the challenge and the intrigue more." That's what he'd kept telling himself to make sense of the senseless violence. "Perhaps it's always been my first love."

"And that's why you'll never allow yourself to love another woman. The hurt and disappointment is more painful than whatever consequences your position brings." Miranda captured his face between her palms. "You poor man."

"It's my life. I've made that choice and will live with it." He slid his hands along her ribcage and then cupped her breasts. With each stroke of his fingers, her nipples hardened. Arousing her served as a distraction from the pain he'd never escape from—didn't know if he wanted to. It was too much a part of him now. If he kept it within himself, he'd never forget, never bring the same bad luck on someone else. He rubbed the pads of his thumbs over the tight buds, and his cock jumped when she responded with a breathy moan. "Do you understand why I don't want more than a physical connection with a woman?"

"I do, but I think you do yourself a disservice."

"It's no more than you're doing by keeping men at arm's length due to the alleged curse."

"We're not talking about me." She tugged him close. Her lips nearly met his. "I think you want to belong to a woman. You want to know you matter to someone. In a tiny, shadowy part of your mind, you want the security that she'll be waiting, and she'll miss and mourn for you if something goes awry." She brushed her lips against his. "You want to make a difference, to leave your mark on the world."

He didn't answer. He couldn't. What would he say? An agreement would reduce his carefully groomed reputation and soften his personality. Falling in love made a man vulnerable. He refused to go through the remainder of his life knowing someone he cared for could be in danger simply from being tied to him. He wouldn't sacrifice a career he loved and was skilled in for a relationship or to be fat and lazy in a domestic capacity, bored to flinders.

"Richard?" She gave him a little shake.

"Don't read too far into my psyche, Miranda. I'm married to my livelihood, and I like it that way. Missions end. I can walk away with no cost to me." He wrapped his hands around her upper arms. "As long as I have a woman available to relieve my cock when I'm home, I'm happy." He held her gaze and refused to puzzle out the emotions clouding her eyes. "This is who I am. You can take what I'm offering, or I can never see you again." Doubt twisted his insides. He didn't want to lose her, but he wanted it clear he couldn't give all she needed.

The beating of his heart was so loud he feared she could hear it. Would she realize how terrified he was, or that every moment spent in her company drew him closer to her regardless of the words he'd just said?

"You can come back to me. I'll be waiting." Miranda wet her lips. "Kiss me." It wasn't an invitation. It was an order.

He took the permission in the spirit in which she'd given it and crushed her into his embrace. Her soft, warm lips welcomed his advance. The clutch of her fingers in the lapels of his jacket gave away her need—a need he intended to exploit. After nudging her lips apart, he thrust his tongue into her mouth, tangling with hers. She fenced with him for several seconds, never giving quarter but taking what she wanted from him. By the time he broke the kiss, it was he who panted with desire, he whose body hummed with lust.

One look at her kiss-swollen lips and into her passion-filled eyes and he was lost. "Oh God." There was nothing he wanted more in that one moment than to bury his shaft deep inside her warmth. He slanted his mouth over hers. Again and again, he explored, seeking to taste her—brand her. When she uttered soft mews of pleasure, he broke the kiss in order to trail his lips along the underside of her jaw. Richard licked a path down the column of her throat then traced her collarbones. A hint of floral soap tinged with the freshness of her skin clung to his tongue and spiked his ardor. He pressed his hips into hers, grinding his engorged member into her belly. That small amount of friction provided little relief and only ramped his resolve.

Miranda slid a hand between them. She stroked his arousal through his breeches, and his member jumped. "Will I need to wonder about your prowess, or will you show me?"

He reeled as if she'd slapped him. "Did you just proposition me?"

"I did." She worked the buttons of his breeches. When the fabric fell open, his heavy length sprang into her hand.

Richard shook with a host of tremors as she stroked her fingers down his member, her palm silky against his skin. "I thought you didn't wish to court scandal." He couldn't think while she worked him. His cock tightened to the point of painfulness.

"It's not a scandal unless we're caught. Isn't that what you keep saying?"

Her mischievous grin sent him over the edge. "Wicked woman." Richard glanced around the room. He didn't want to use the settee again, as it hadn't been comfortable the last time they'd indulged. Urgency demanded he solve the problem soon.

Quickly, before she could voice a protest or change her mind, he spun her around and bent her over the plush curve of the crushed velvet settee. "I've waited for this moment ever since John first told me about you." He shoved her skirts up, bunching them about her waist until her bare arse was revealed.

"This is hardly proper." Miranda scrambled to maintain her balance in her precarious position and eventually lost the fight. Her front half pitched downward, and she braced herself with her hands on the seat.

"Neither is a *ménage a trois* but this will determine if you, John and I will proceed with one." He smoothed his hands over her satiny buttocks. What would she do if he spanked her a few times and colored those pale globes with pink? Perhaps another time. "You were made to be pleasured, Miranda."

"Not for a man's pleasure?"

"Oh no. You deserve to be sent flying by a man's fingers, mouth, and cock, and often." He slid a hand between her thighs. "Women like you should always be flushed from finding release and sated from being cherished." He drew a finger along her folds already slick with desire. "Spread your legs, love. Let me get you good and wet before I fuck you."

She did as he asked without question or protest, almost as if she'd reserve judgment until he performed.

Richard grinned as he rubbed his fingers along her slippery flesh. There'd be no need to tease or play. She was ready for him. Yet he couldn't help fondling her flesh or circling her nub with a fingertip. Her body shook. A moan escaped her. She struggled to stand upright. He wouldn't let her, keeping her in place with a hand at the small of her back. "What do you want, Miranda?" He tormented her button with quick passes of his fingers, coating it with her juices.

She wriggled her hips in response. "You already know."

Seeing her naked rear end in the air and feeling her moisture gripped Richard more than he'd anticipated. He withdrew his hand from her thighs only to completely free his aching cock from his breeches. "I'll wager this is it." He guided his member through her essence and then pushed into her heat.

Damn it all but she was so hot and snug. He withdrew and thrust back in merely to experience the wonder of penetration once more. Miranda uttered a long, low moan. She shoved backward and impaled herself fully on his hard cock. His balls rubbed against her pink skin and set off a host of intense sensations. If he didn't take control of the situation, he'd spend before he was ready, yet he loved she had the experience to know how to position him.

Richard gripped her hips, anchored her to the settee and set a quick rhythm of short, forceful strokes. Each one sent him deep into her passage. Each one shot need up his shaft and all through his body. As he watched his length slide into her channel, his balls and sac warmed with intense feeling, but he continued to move. The wet slap of flesh filled his ears, punctuated by Miranda's moans. He gritted his teeth. At this rate he wouldn't last. How could he help it when she was so wonderfully pleasing?

"Give into it." He slipped a hand around her hip to fondle her button. His heart raced. Sweat coated his back, soaking through his shirt. His cock pulsed. Release was imminent. "Let me hear you." The prompt wasn't needed as his name on a scream left her lips. God, how he adored hearing that sound. The widow was well and truly his. Tremors gripped his member, increasing in strength and volume as she squirmed. "That's right. Ride it."

He took hold of her hips once more. His thrusting became more frantic. He went long and deep into her body, and when his release finally came, his breath caught. Strong and swift, pleasure raced through his cock and ebbed outward. His seed shot into her with each pulse of his member, and her inner walls greedily milked him dry.

Before his strength gave out completely, he pulled Miranda into a standing position and held her tight against him, her back to his front. He rained kisses onto her nape. Her heartbeat fluttered beneath his lips. Slight tremors racked her body. "Please tell me I can see you again before I leave for France."

"Yes." She brought one of his hands to her lips and kissed it. "I'm throwing a small fete on Sunday. Come. We'll discuss things at that time." Her voice had taken on a dreamy quality, and she went pliant in his arms.

"I'll try to control myself until then." Bloody hell, it would be difficult. His chest tightened. Despite his best intentions to keep whatever was between them to sex only, he'd lost a piece of his soul to her the moment she ordered him to kiss her.

What does that mean for our future and why do I feel I might break her heart?

Chapter Nine

Miranda couldn't contain her smug grin, even after she'd knotted her embroidery thread for the second time. Her body was warm and sated after the rushed coupling with Richard. Now, he sat on a chair opposite hers, reading the morning paper. Remarkably, he'd consented to stay on for a proper visit and didn't seem willing to leave any time soon. She loved the easy domestic atmosphere almost as much as she enjoyed the companionable silence they shared. It didn't matter that he'd never give his heart to her; what he had shared was sweet enough, and she had flirted in an effort to force his hand. Knowing John would undoubtedly come around again and make things right kept the smile on her lips. She did hold him in high regard, but he did need to understand she wouldn't give up her identity in order to be with him.

She peeked at Richard, but his face remained hidden behind the paper. Miranda laid the handiwork in her lap and bit her bottom lip. There simply was nothing as heavenly as feeling a man's thick, engorged cock filling her passage and teasing her inner walls or hitting that secret spot inside with just enough pressure to send her flying. She'd missed that intimacy since her last husband died, missed the close connection to a man.

In the remembering, moisture tickled her feminine curls and need tingled through her breasts, weighting them. She hadn't indulged in physical relations for more than two years yet now in the space of a couple days, she'd enjoyed the same with two men.

And what was more, it hadn't been nearly enough to satisfy her appetite. A tiny giggle escaped her. *Perhaps I am as voracious as Mrs. Stowe claimed.*

Richard had been so different from John. Where Richard preferred short, forceful thrusts, John had pleasured her with long, slow strokes, but both had seen her through to release in mere moments. Both men had made her feel safe and desired, but would either want to reside on her estate in Surrey in order to win her, and if they both did, how could their relationship withstand the public eye and certain scandal? Would there be enough between all of them to build a satisfying life upon after the heat of passion faded?

The residual euphoric feelings vanished in the face of the stark reality she considered. *I refuse to be their affair of the moment. I want... more. I'd like to have them for a lifetime, but how can I with the curse?* How could she enjoy such a thing when marrying again would doom the man whose name she legally took, and what of the second gentleman? She couldn't very well wed both, but would her back luck curse him as well? "Oh, bother." Not to mention she'd dismissed John in haste and without letting him explain himself. She'd need to patch that up if they were to continue. *I acted abominably with him.*

"Woman, if you stare at me with questions and a come-hither invitation, I will ravish you again." Richard lowered the paper and laid a smoldering gaze on her. "What troubles you?"

She dropped her embroidery into a basket at her feet. "I'm marveling that a handful of days ago, I lived a content lifestyle here alone. Now my home has been literally besieged by you and John; my feelings usurped. I'm wondering how I can divide my time between two men and still maintain my identity, respectability and sanity."

"Sometimes, living free means not thinking about how to be content. Those feelings come if the situation is right without you needing to do anything." Richard lifted an eyebrow. "However, if you require more convincing, I'd be happy to oblige."

A shiver raced down Miranda's spine. The dark shadows in his eyes promised nights full of wickedness. "Look who's found his mischief again."

"I never lost it, my dear."

She rose from her chair, fully intent on indulging in passing a few minutes in passionate kisses when a sharp rap on the door banished the thought. "Damnation. Can I not have a moment's peace anymore?" Instead of joining Richard, she crossed the room, unlocked the door then pulled it open to admit Eppson. "What now?" Her annoyance toward her butler hadn't dissipated. She didn't care for his penchant of weeding her callers without her permission.

Eppson drew himself to his full height. "I beg your pardon for the interruption, Mrs. Craythorne, but Lady Underhill is here with questions regarding your matchmaking services. Will you attend her in the parlor or shall I show her into your conservatory?"

"Do I not have the right to make the decision if I shall see her at all?" Her displeasure increased tenfold. Of course, Lady Underhill was a huge influence in Surrey, and if she truly desired to use Miranda's matching services, it would be quite a feather in the cap of her fledging business. Her shoulders drooped. "Fine. Show her in here since I am still enjoying Mr. Howick's visit."

"Very good, ma'am." Eppson bowed then retreated down the hall.

Miranda faced Richard. "I apologize for the interruption. I hope you don't mind." By the time she'd crossed the room and resettled into her abandoned chair, he'd folded the paper and cast it aside.

"Not in the least. I can charm the formidable dragon if you wish." He wore a naughty expression. "I'm told no lady can withstand me when I'm bent on winning her over."

Her heart squeezed. "I'm sure this is true, but won't be necessary. I'm well-versed in Lady Underhill's tactics. Chances are she's merely nosy. Or, she feels the need to give me a warning in person since Mrs. Stowe's advice didn't help."

"Ah, and of course, you are entertaining a gentleman alone—again." His grin smacked of trouble making. "That must mean you're doing something scandalous."

A rush of heat swept through her body. "Well, wasn't I?"

"Indeed." He leaned forward in his chair, and with a flourish, withdrew a small, rectangular object from a pocket of his tailcoat. "I have a gift for you."

"What is it?" Flutters filled her stomach. It had been an age since she'd received a gift from a suitor.

"Silly goose. Take it and see." He waved the box at her, chuckling when she accepted it.

"It's a beautiful... snuff box?" She frowned. "But I don't indulge in such a habit and neither do I collect such containers." Miranda traced the brown-and-green enameled surface. It was inlaid with shells that glowed in the sunlight. "It's lovely, though."

"It's merely a receptacle for the real treasure inside." His smug expression set her insides on fire. "Open it."

She did and gazed upon tight little green balls resembling pearls. "What is it?" She held the box to her nose and sniffed. A faint floral aroma danced across her senses.

"My dear, I have managed to procure you a rare oolong tea straight from the growers in Taiwan. Normally, the Chinese have very strict control over such a delicacy, but through my more unsavory connections, I purchased this in London yesterday thinking you might enjoy it."

"Why?"

Richard shrugged. "You were on my mind. Why not?"

And here he'd just said he'd not commit to a woman again. Miranda sucked in a breath. "You had it smuggled into England?" She couldn't wait to sample it. How would it be different than the tea she drank every day?

"Not me. Someone else did. I merely purchased it on the black market here, thereby bypassing the steep taxes levied by the East India Company." His grin widened. "I choose not to buy into their control of the tea line." He looked so pleased with himself, she couldn't help but match his smile.

"Thank you." Tears misted her eyes. He'd thought of her while he'd been away. He'd bought an exotic tea to please her.

She blinked at the moisture. "It's perhaps the best gift anyone has ever given me, and I'll treasure it." Carefully, she closed the lid and then set the snuff box on the table beside her.

"I hope you'll brew it and drink it. That's the best treasure."

"I will, and think of you each time." She had no opportunity to say more for a rap on the doorframe sounded and then Eppson announced Lady Underhill. Miranda rose as the stalwart woman sailed into the room. "Hello, Lady Underhill." For the life of her she couldn't remember the woman's first name so overwhelmed had she been by Richard's kindness. She'd much rather throw herself into his arms and kiss him until she'd thanked him properly.

"Good day, Mrs. Craythorne." The baron's wife nodded. The silk flowers on her wide-brimmed hat bobbed from the effort. "Who is this?" She shot a bold glance at Richard, who rose as well.

"Lady Underhill, this is Mr. Richard Howson." Miranda's stomach clenched as they stared at each other. What kind of vitriol would spew from Lady Underhill this time? Could the lady guess what had transpired between Richard and her?

"A pleasure." Richard's voice rumbled through the frosty silence. He uttered a small sigh when Lady Underhill sat on the settee between the chairs. "I trust you don't mind my presence." He returned to his chair and laid an ankle on a knee.

"Not at all." A simper contorted Lady Underhill's fat face. Her beady eyes gleamed. "Though I did mean to talk with Miranda about her matchmaking, I find I'm curious about you, sir. What do you do for a living and why are you hanging about in Miranda's home with nary a chaperone?"

Miranda gaped at her visitor as she resumed her seat. How dare she inquire about things which didn't concern her? "Lady Underhill, perhaps Mr. Howick would rather—"

"No, it's quite a legitimate question." Richard interrupted. All humor had gone from his expression, replaced with barely veiled anger. He narrowed his eyes as he regarded Lady Underhill. "I work for the Home Office, but I'm afraid I cannot reveal exactly what I do as that is privileged information."

"I see." The baron's wife rearranged her light blue skirts. "And you are here to discuss what? Military secrets?" When silence met her question, she harrumphed, sounding much like the trumpet of an elephant. "Being an upstanding member of country society, I'm concerned Miranda's penchant for... entertaining as she has in recent days will corrupt our young people. Why, just yesterday, a different man was seen exiting her home. This same man had been spotted climbing out of her parlor window a few days ago."

Heat suffused Miranda's cheeks. "Have you been monitoring me, Lady Underhill? For that's the only way you could have seen any activity near my house as the trees and surrounding park land obscure a view from the road." Did she, even now, have someone on the property spying on her? She pressed a hand to her chest. Dear heavens, had someone seen her and John in the stillroom? The thought left her cold.

"I think for the good of our village, someone needs to be aware of what the neighbors are doing." She'd neither confirmed nor denied the accusation. "Now, Mr. Howson, what exactly is your business with Mrs. Craythorne?"

Miranda met his gaze and shrugged, still stunned by the attack. Behind them, the budgies had gone quiet, but the cockatoo screeched a few times. She glanced at the bird. His yellow crest stood to full attention while he bobbed his head. Clearly he didn't care for the visitor.

Richard rubbed a hand along his jaw. "Quite frankly, it's none of your concern why I'm here, Lady Underhill. The last time I checked, I didn't need to ask permission before visiting someone other than you." He shot to his feet, his eyes flashing. "Also, both Miranda and I are adults, even consenting adults if you want to know. What we do in the privacy of these walls is not your business, but as you can see, we were doing nothing more than enjoying a quiet at-home before your arrival."

"That doesn't explain the appearance of the other gentleman." Lady Underhill's double chins wobbled with her indignation.

"Nor will there be an explanation." Miranda stood. She'd finally found her voice. From the deadly glint in Richard's eye, he seemed ready to commit murder right there in her conservatory, not that she blamed him. Lady Underhill's interference was outside of enough. "Lady Underhill, if you wish to discuss matchmaking, so be it. Everything else is private and not your concern."

"I should say it is. The village doesn't need a loose woman on their doorstep, especially if you're trying to use our little society as a base for your matchmaking services." She pinned Richard with a glare. "And you, young man, should watch yourself. You may be a rake and a rogue in London, but here in Surrey, we keep to a more strict set of morals. If you persist in being a cad, I'll convince the local authorities to come calling. Imagine what trouble Mrs. Craythorne would find then."

"Now, that's enough, Lady Underhill. You overstep." Richard curled a hand into a fist. When Miranda lifted an eyebrow, he relaxed his stance slightly. "Perhaps it's time for me to go. I do have a pressing appointment elsewhere that really cannot wait."

"Oh, Richard, please stay. I'm certain Lady Underhill's visit is nearly over." Of course it was. The woman only came to deliver her veiled warning, especially since Mrs. Stowe's words of advice hadn't had an effect, just as Miranda had predicted. It was probably a feather in the baroness's cap that she happened to catch Richard as well.

He held her gaze. His roiled with emotions she couldn't—or wouldn't—name. He yanked his hat and gloves from the empty chair. "I'd rather not sully our time together by doing or saying something I'll regret later." He strode across the room so fast his coattails flapped behind him.

Miranda followed in his wake and stopped him at the door with a hand on his arm. "Please don't come the crab over her. She's vile to everyone and not worth it."

A small grin softened his face but didn't reach his eyes. "There's only so much a man can take before he needs an outlet for his ire. I'd rather go out riding or shoot pheasant. Otherwise, it might be too tempting to shoot her." He patted her hand. "Thank you for your time this morning." His eyes darkened. "I appreciated your words and the use of your body."

She nodded. Her throat tightened. He hadn't mentioned anything about forever or even affection. Would he have if Lady Underhill hadn't called and destroyed their pleasant morning? But he'd given her the tea gift. That had to mean something. "Please come to my soiree tomorrow evening. It'll be a nice way to send you off before work claims you." She dropped her voice. "I'd rather not have you return to the field without being able to assure you a place to come home to." Dear heavens, that wasn't what she'd wanted to say, but she couldn't kiss him as she wished with Lady Underhill looking on. Miranda sighed. When would her life be her own? "The musicale portion of the evening will begin at nine with dinner at eleven. Cards and other entertainment will be available as well."

Richard leaned close and whispered in her ear, "If I have my way, the entertainment I have in mind will be conducted in private with much moaning. I care naught for any other sounds." Without another word, he quit the room and didn't look back.

A shiver racked her body. She ran her hands up and down her arms before finally turning to Lady Underhill. "Will there be anything else?"

The stout baron's wife stood. She shook the wrinkles from her gown. "Your behavior is quite scandalous, even for a widow, Miranda. That display just now was very shocking."

And that was mere conversation. "I have no idea what you mean." Miranda traversed the perimeter of the room and headed toward her birdcages. "Where is the harm in being courted? If I was a debutante and had the interest of two eligible men, no one would say a thing. In fact, I'd be lauded as a success, but since I've been a widow, I wonder why everyone is inordinately interested in my romances?"

Lady Underhill sniffed. "That isn't the issue."

"Perhaps you should explain in very specific words then. I'm rather fatigued at the moment." She allowed a small smile. Being put through her paces by Richard earlier had indeed brought on a bout of tiredness.

"This village won't stand for the wicked ways you indulge in. Two men, Miranda? It's scandal enough to conduct an affair with one, but two? You're simply asking for trouble."

"Then you'll be happy to know I haven't started an affair yet, and I can say with all honesty, I haven't seen either man naked." To her credit, her lips didn't twitch—not even once. Yes, she'd experienced relations with both of them, but they'd yet to shed their clothes. "You needn't worry about me."

"Oh, I'm not worried. I know what sort of woman you are, which is why I've kept my sons well away." Lady Underhill narrowed her eyes. "I'll caution you that reputations can be ruined in moments. You should watch your step, Mrs. Craythorne. I know how much this property means to you, even if it does belong to your brother. I'd hate for you to need to leave in a rush based on assumptions and rumors."

Miranda's stomach twisted. A sick feeling rose in her throat tasting of bitter bile. She clenched a hand in her skirt. Lady Underhill commanded a huge amount of respect and power in the local community as well as the whole of Surrey. Should she heed the warning and try to shield both John and Richard from the woman's ire? What about herself? "Is that a threat, Lady Underhill?"

"Not at all. I'm merely stating my concern for the village, and for your future, of course."

A headache pounded behind Miranda's eyes as she considered her options. How could one brief meeting on a terrace have brought her to such a pass where she needed to worry about destroying the reputations of men she'd come to care for? She forced a swallow. "Perhaps, Lady Underhill, you should mind your own business before you start mucking around in mine. After all, didn't your daughter cause a scandal right under your nose not too long ago?"

Lady Underhill's face blanched. Her chins trembled. "How dare you see fit to mention my daughter in the same subject as your indiscretions?"

Miranda shrugged. "From where I'm standing, there's not much difference. A scandal is a scandal, all in the eyes of the law and the God-fearing. It's how one conducts themselves within it that makes the difference."

The baroness swept across the room. Every bulge and roll of fat brimmed with her anger. "Have a care, Mrs. Craythorne. You never know who is watching." She left the room and the tap-tap of her heels on the title floor rang in the absence.

"Dear heavens what a foul woman." As the strength fled her limbs, Miranda sank to the floor. Her heart pounded against her ribcage. *What should I do now?* If protecting the men meant she had to lose them, would she have the strength to do it?

Chapter Ten

Miranda stood on the terrace, looking into the drawing room where a string triplet and a young lady playing the pianoforte performed. She enjoyed the song selections they'd picked; each one tugged at her soul to tap her foot or made her want to dance, which is what she'd much rather do. Unfortunately, there wasn't enough room for dancing as she hadn't planned for it. The guest list only boasted at most twenty people—thirty since some of the invitees had brought friends or escorts. She'd asked close friends and family in the hope that having the people she liked best around her would help prompt a decision. Plus, she still intended to match her cousin and had specifically invited several eligible men for the purpose. Dancing aside, the men milling about her home didn't interest her. She wanted John and Richard, needed their strength and humor to lift her spirits, but neither of the gentlemen had arrived.

Unless that dratted Eppson has run them off. A twinge of panic twisted up her spine. She would need to lecture him on the proper behavior of servants, but it would be a hopeless cause. The governing of her heavy-handed servants from years of relying on them as friends had become a mess.

She snapped her attention back to the room. Doris Stowe, the minister's wife who'd bedeviled her earlier in the week, sat in a chair at the back of the room, for all intents and purposes enjoying herself. She listened to the music with a rapt expression on her face. Miranda smiled. She'd purposefully invited the woman so Doris could see for herself there was no need to fear for Miranda's soul. The fact she'd accepted then subsequently appeared meant Miranda was still in the local community's good graces despite the veiled warnings.

Now, as boredom and wistfulness crept through her, Miranda turned and retreated once more into the shadows on the terrace. Light spilled from both drawing rooms creating golden pools on the flagstones. While a handful of people lingered on the terrace taking the air or simply talking in low murmurs, a few couples strolled the garden paths. Had she ruined her chance with John? And if so, what would happen to her liaison with Richard? She doubted they'd even have that since he was due to leave for his mission tomorrow and it was obvious John was the glue holding them all together. He kept Richard from getting out of hand and eased her fears. Richard had promised to temper John's overprotective instincts. John's goal had never wavered since he'd come to Surrey. Both men needed each other for balance. She needed them for the same in her life. Perhaps rusticating was fine, but the men had brought excitement and a spark she'd been missing.

Yet, doubt still held her in its grip. *Why does everything have to be so difficult?*

She rested her forearms on the cool stone railing and fixed her gaze on the moonlit garden paths. Such an idyllic scene for romance. Somewhere in the distance, a screech from a peacock broke the night's stillness. The birds had bedded down, but occasionally one would take exception to the guests on the property, even though they were nowhere near the muster. *Silly peacocks.* She sympathized with them. Her own home had been interrupted by Richard and John and she still wanted to squawk and shoo them off her property so she'd be left alone—in order to spare them and keep her own identity intact. But then, she'd be... alone, and oh, how could she abide that? Separately and combined, the two had made an indelible impression on her.

"You have the look of a woman conflicted. I hope I'm not the one who put that frown on your delectable lips."

At the sound of the deep voice she'd longed to hear since the night began, she spun. "John." Her heart beat a frantic rhythm. He stood close, magnificent in dark evening clothes, his shoulders broad and his form filling his jacket to perfection. "I thought you'd chosen not to come." His black curls gleamed in the soft light while a shadow of stubble clung to his strong jaw lending him a rugged, mysterious persona. A sapphire stick pin winked from the snowy folds of his cravat.

"Never. How could I pass on an opportunity to try and win your heart one last time?"

Did that mean he wouldn't ask again if she refused him tonight? Miranda swallowed to moisten her dry throat. She couldn't lose him. This night was for firm decisions. "I'm glad."

Another step brought him to her side. "You're lovely this evening. That gown suits you."

"Oh pish-posh." Warmth skated through her insides as she smoothed a hand down the front of her gown. She'd chosen a black silk frock decorated with black lace and jet beads. Paired with a ruffled orange satin duster jacket and matching slippers, she'd hoped the combination would lend her confidence and be striking enough that John couldn't ignore her.

"It's true. Not many women would be so daring with their color choices. Only you, love. I adore your adventurous spirit."

She sighed when he grasped her hand then trembled as he swept her into a modified embrace, much like he'd do if they were to indulge in dancing. This was what she'd been waiting for; he was the man she wanted, and if she could only have him for the night, then she wouldn't argue with fate. Right now, he was hers. "I'm sorry for my behavior the other day. I should never have listened to Annabelle. I was afraid—"

"Hush, Miranda. There's nothing to apologize for. Emotions ran high that afternoon. We shall talk before this evening is over. There is still much to decide." He winked. "May I have this dance?"

She glanced around the terrace. A couple of people looked their way as if to see what they'd do, but she didn't care. This was her house and her party. The need to be near John was much stronger than her worry about convention. "Yes, please." Tendrils of heat curled in her lower belly and streaked between her thighs. Oh how she'd missed him during the days he'd stayed away. With John, everything seemed more brilliant.

Then her world narrowed to include only him. The strains of the music faded. She melted into his arms and pressed herself as close as he would allow, which wasn't enough. Her guests prevented intimacy. His clean scent wafted around her. The warmth from his body seeped into hers; the strength of his hands as he held her brought her comfort and made her feel protected. She didn't utter a word. She couldn't, not when the reality of holding John close stole her ability to talk as well as breathe. The chill from the air kissed her overheated skin while she held his gaze and let him sweep her down the length of the terrace. In that one moment she believed she was like other women and could look forward to living out the rest of her days beside a man without causing his early demise.

"Is this a private dance or may I steal the fair lady away?"

John released her and gently gave her into Richard's keeping. "If the venue was more private, the three of us could enjoy a dance of another kind, but since it's not, I have no qualms letting you enjoy more conventional exercise—as long as she returns to me soon." His whispered rejoinder sent shivers over her skin.

She trembled as Richard held her close with a hand at the small of her back, much closer than John had done, but then, Richard was the more daring of the pair. "Richard. You're here too." He was just as handsome in evening clothes as John, but his leaner frame and shorter height made him seem less imposing and somewhat more approachable—until she caught his gaze, which glittered with wicked intent. Tension wound taut in his body. She felt it beneath her fingers. Had he come with a specific purpose in mind? Gooseflesh popped on her exposed skin. Moisture tickled between her thighs. Of course he had, and oh how she wanted to experience that.

A couple bumped into her as they danced past, and Richard took the excuse to hold her. She and John had apparently set an example and inadvertently opened impromptu dancing on the terrace.

"How could I not come?" He put his lips to her ear as he waltzed. His thin mustache tickled her temple and heighted her need. "My last night in England should be spent in the perfumed arms of a woman. I want that woman to be you, in as many ways I can imagine."

"Oh." She tightened her hand in his. Could he feel her shaking? His exotic, spicy scent increased her hunger. She'd already experienced the feel of each of their cocks, quick though each meeting had been. What would his body look like without the clothes? How different would he be from how she imagined John's form? How would the men work together to pleasure her? "I'd like that, but I'd prefer both you and John in my bed. This time I want to be loved in a proper place."

Love. Was that what she desired from them both? Could they give it, or did they merely want the physical, and could she give them every part of herself without condition regardless of what they offered?

Richard chuckled. He slid a hand to the curve of her rear and gave her a pinch. "That can be arranged." His dark eyes winked with promise in the faint light.

"Never say you two are plotting without me." John met them at the opposite railing and halted their twirling with a hand on Miranda's arm.

"More like plotting about you—or at least using you in conjunction to Miranda's nefarious purposes." Richard urged her out of his embrace, so she stood between them, not quite touching but close enough that the heat from both men singed her bare arms. Her nipples beaded and her breasts ached for the men's attention.

"Oh? What has our matchmaker planned?"

Miranda glanced from one of their dear faces to the other. It would be a good hour or so until dinner was served, yet her guests were free to move about the house as they pleased since it wasn't a formal event. While it was true that no one would necessarily miss her if she wanted to drag the men into a secluded nook and indulge in a light seduction—a prelude to bedroom delights—the added excitement of perhaps being discovered added mystery and urgency to the situation. It was a heady tease indeed. She grabbed a hand of each man. "You'll need to come with me to find out."

Her pulse rushed in her ears as she led them into the drawing room. Once across the threshold, she released their hands as it wouldn't do to blatantly advertise her intent, plus they couldn't very well walk three abreast through the door. With each step she pictured their naked bodies in her mind with their taut muscles and engorged cocks, aroused exclusively for her. Her breath came in shallow pants, but she smiled at a few acquaintances, even went so far as to wave at Annabelle before gaining the hallway door. She felt their presence as she followed the hall toward the east wing of the house and there pushed open the door to a defunct study.

The room had belonged to her brother when he'd used the estate. Since then, she'd left the slipcovers on the furniture to protect the pieces from dust. She much preferred her conservatory to this room. The lamps weren't burning as she never opened the study to visitors and heavy shadows crowded the ceiling and corners. No sooner had she stepped inside than John caught her in his arms and fitted his mouth over hers—hot, wet, and determined.

Miranda moaned against his lips from the sheer wonder of experiencing his kiss again. She locked her arms around his shoulders and surrendered, meeting every stroke and thrust of his tongue with one of her own. He slid his hands to her waist and ground his hips into hers. The hard length of his erection rubbed her stomach. Tingles and heat filled her body. She wrenched away and sought out his gaze in the dark. "John..."

He held her head between his big palms and fanned his fingers into her hair. "I was a fool the other day, Miranda. I should have fought harder, told your damn butler and cousin to bugger off." His warm breath caressed her cheek. "Hell, I should have ordered them away."

Threads of annoyance trickled through her chest. "You're not the master here." Though she'd delivered a gentle reminder, she didn't have the heart to give him a further set down.

"Not yet." John brushed her mouth with butterfly kisses. He nibbled at her bottom lip. Each tiny nip had desire building in her core.

The annoyance soon turned to anticipation. Would he master her as well if she let him in fully?

Richard came behind her and grasped her hips. He rubbed his thumbs over the small of her back, branding her. "He can be; we both can." He drew a line of searing kisses along her nape. "Let us master you—here, the bedroom, or anywhere else you should desire, as many times as you'd like. This night is for your pleasure."

Need zipped through her belly. It lanced through her passage and pulsed between her legs. "Not until after dinner. I'll be missed..." As Richard slid his hands upward to cup her breasts, Miranda let her anxiety go. He worried her nipples through the satin of her gown, coaxing them into aching peaks. She gasped. John pressed her closer and insinuated a knee between her thighs, all the while plundering her mouth.

Richard encouraged her forward, so she leaned on John's leg, and she went, having no extra strength to protest. The friction against her nub sent awareness throughout her body. Her thighs quivered. It took all her willpower not to grind on him like a wanton. She pulled slightly away. "Dear heavens, you two are potent."

"We're only just starting." Richard pinched her nipples. He dipped a hand into her bodice, his fingers warm on her skin as he palmed a breast. "Shall we continue?"

Miranda moaned her consent. She arched her back, giving Richard better access, and her button rubbed harder against John's leg. The heated tingles between her thighs increased. Was it possible to reach release without either of them directly touching her center?

"Good Lord, Miranda! What are you doing?"

As if a bucket of water had been thrown on her, passion cooled at the sound of her cousin's voice. Annabelle's shock ricocheted through Miranda's head, and she pulled away from the men though her breathing continued to rasp. She blinked against the sudden onslaught of light from the candles both Annabelle and Mrs. Stowe, who stood behind her cousin, held. "Annabelle, what are you doing here?" Had the girl followed her? Were there others in the hall? Miranda couldn't discern if it was so as the candlelight played tricks with her vision.

The minister's wife's eyes were as round as saucers. Her jaw was agape. "Dear heavens, such depravity. The rumors are true." She backed out of the room. Her hand shook and the candle flame danced, casting macabre shadows on the walls. "I must leave immediately." She fled down the hall.

Both John and Richard closed ranks. They each laid a hand on her arm. John cleared his throat. "Is there a problem, Miss Lythe?"

Annabelle pressed her lips into a thin line. She glanced between the men before pinning Miranda with a look brimming with disappointment and shocked disgust. "Cousin, I could throw my support behind you if you were merely conducting an affair with Mr. Goddard. That smacked of star-crossed romance, and I would have been proud to brag about our connection, but this," she gestured at them, "this is something else entirely."

"Let me explain." Miranda pitched forward, a hand outstretched.

"No." Annabelle backed away. "I can no longer associate with you. I have my own reputation and future to think about, don't you see?" Tears pooled in her eyes. "How could you even think to damage that for me?"

She ignored the question. "Why is what I can have with Mr. Goddard and Mr. Howson any different than merely conducting an affair with John only?" The way her cousin stared at her as if she'd sprouted feathers sent waves of guilt over her. Old familiar prickles of fear mixed with humiliation climbed her throat.

"You could have married John and made the rumors go away. Now, with three, it's impossible and immoral. It cannot be done, Miranda."

"They make me happy. Why can I not have that? Why is it wrong?" Was that her voice pleading? Never had she been reduced to near whining.

"It just is. There are rules. Society is strict. You know this." Annabelle sniffed. Her chin trembled. "I'm sorry."

Miranda nodded, but her cousin had already quit the room. The *tap-tap* of her heels on the wood faded as she put distance between them. "Well, that's that." Bands of sadness and failure crushed her chest. Not even the gentle pressure of John's hand on her back calmed the knots in her stomach. "I suppose the damage is just starting." It was a matter of time now before the news circulated through the gathering and then spread onward into the village.

Why can't I have the love of family, friends, and my men?

John's heart ached for Miranda, but he held himself together until a single tear fell to her cheek. The euphoria from minutes before vanished under a blanket of seething anger. It would take several more minutes before his engorged cock settled back to normal. Had they not been interrupted, all three of them would have ended in a tangled heap on the floor. "I'm sorry, love." He bundled her into his arms and pressed a kiss into her hair. "Don't let the opinions of small-minded people tarnish your opinion of yourself or quell the joy you've found."

"He's quite correct." Richard stroked a hand down her back. "If we truly make you happy, why worry about anyone else?"

"A week ago, I was happy *here*, with my plants and my birds, and then you two came along and shook that happiness. You made it bigger, broader, expanded it into something I dared not hope for, into something I'm not sure I deserve."

John's coat and cravat muffled her words. "Now everything I once knew and found comfort in is threatened."

"We're going to face whatever happens together." John put her at arm's length. He hoped his tone and expression conveyed his intent. "Understand?"

Miranda nodded.

"All three of us." Richard turned her to face him. "If your friends and family cannot stick by you for everything, you don't need them." He cupped her face with both hands. "John and I will never abandon you." He brushed his lips to hers. "Thick or thin."

John nodded. He tucked a fallen tendril of hair behind her ear. "Go mingle among your guests. We'll follow in a few moments. Your cousin might not tattle due to the taint of scandal, but Mrs. Stowe probably couldn't wait to spread the gossip. You might walk away unscathed—if you're lucky." But he knew the sad reality of the situation. This did not bode well for any of them.

"That would assume I walk with something other than misfortune as a companion." Miranda pulled away, but the pallor of her expression betrayed her worry. "I've faced the tabbies before. This should be old hat." She inclined her chin and straightened her spine before setting off.

Once she'd left the room, John shoved a hand through his hair. "This has devastating potential." That minister's wife had looked ready to vomit on their shoes with Miss Lythe not far behind. "It could tip Miranda away from us."

"It cannot be worse than facing the French when they're in a snit." Richard clapped a hand on John's shoulder. "Stiff upper lip and all that. We'll make do."

"Let's not bugger it up this time. I'm quite tired of being on the defensive." John quit the room. The thud of Richard's boots behind him confirmed his friend trailed.

Thick, pregnant silence hit him the moment he entered the foyer. People stood in random pockets of twos and threes, all whispering, some female faces hidden behind their fans. Each pair of eyes followed him and Richard. He stood straighter upon seeing Miss Lythe. She lingered off to one side. A blush colored her face, and she averted her eyes when he would have met her gaze. John grunted. His gut clenched. *Something is afoot.* Soft strains of the string musicians reached his ears. Obviously, someone had instructed them to continue to play, perhaps for a sense of normalcy. He strode in Miss Lythe's direction.

"I hope you're happy with yourself, Miss Lythe."

She startled then shrank backward at his approach. "I'm sure I have no idea what you mean, Mr. Goddard."

"Oh, no?" Though he wanted to throttle the woman, he conquered the urge. "I would have thought you'd have stood by Miranda's side, at least in front of her guests. I can excuse much in the face of human nature except the lack of integrity."

Her blush deepened. Tears glimmered in her eyes. "At least I'm decent. What Miranda was doing... what she's done..." Miss Lythe shook her head. "It's embarrassing and will taint my chances for making a match."

What fustian and nonsense. John unclenched his jaw as he considered his next words. "At least your cousin is happy—or was. Why is that so bad?"

Miss Lythe pressed a hand to her throat. "Perhaps she doesn't deserve such a thing if it comes at such a cost."

"The cost being enjoying the attention of two men, or are you concerned for her soul?" Rage slammed into John so great it stole his breath. He counted to ten, curled a hand into a fist before forcing himself to relax. "For that matter, where is Mrs. Stowe?" If he could just talk to the minister's wife before she made the rounds...

"I saw her speaking with Lady Underhill in the foyer not two minutes ago."

"Oh? I find it hard to believe Miranda invited the baroness." Not to something as intimate as this get-together.

Miss Lythe shrugged. "I was of the opinion she'd only just arrived."

Devil take it! Of course the woman would go clucking to the area's biggest troublemaker. And how convenient that woman arrived right at this moment. "Go home, Miss Lythe. Later, perhaps you can reconcile with Miranda, but if you cannot, I warn you not to darken her door again. She has enough obstacles in her path right now in the form of small-minded gentry. She doesn't need the disdain from her own blood." He took his leave of Miranda's cousin, hoping he'd never have cause to see her again.

No matter how hard he searched, he saw no sign of Miranda. The second he stepped into the drawing room, a low rumble of excited talk cycled through the gathering as all eyes turned on him. "Botheration." However, there was no flash of orange satin. He backed out, nearly running into Richard. "Check the conservatory."

Where the hell had she gotten off to? The Miranda he knew would never run from public censure. She'd stand up and fight for her right to live her own way. He curled a hand into a fist.

None of the people around him met his gaze. Some went so far as to turn their backs to him. *Damn bunch of fools. So much for being her closest friends and family.* "Why do you continue to take advantage of Mrs. Craythorne's hospitality by treating her as if she has the plague? She's been nothing but kind to you." He shook his head as he plowed through the onlookers. "The lot of you are cowards." Desperate to track her, he headed toward the parlor where she'd received him the first times he'd visited.

Eppson hovered by the door to the rear parlor, with his hands clasped behind his back. By the time John approached, the butler stood more firmly in the frame.

"Where is Mrs. Craythorne?"

The butler glared. "She is in the parlor, Mr. Goddard, with the constable, but—"

The constable? Damnation but events had moved too quickly for this to be a pleasant, social call. There hadn't been enough time since Mrs. Stowe had caught them all unaware then subsequently tattle to Lady Underhill for the lawman to be summoned. He narrowed his eyes. How long had the local tabbies been plotting to tear Miranda from grace, and had they planned this visit all along regardless of events from earlier in the evening? "I swear, Eppson, if you tell me one more time I cannot see her, I'll bloody your nose. See if I don't." John didn't wait for an answer. He shoved past the fuming butler and entered the parlor. Miranda sat on a settee, her back to the fireplace, while a short, squat man dressed in a dark suit of natty tweed, stood nearby. The material strained across his paunchy belly. Was it the fellow's best clothes? An ambiguous and slightly tarnished badge rested on one lapel. John stifled a snicker. Probably nothing more than an accommodation given in his youth. "What is going on here?"

The man came forward and offered his hand. Dark smudges beneath his eyes grew. "Evening, sir. I'm Constable Barnes. I was told there was some ugly business afoot here that needed to be cleared." His bushy red mustache quivered while a bead of sweat dripped from an equally bushy sideburn. "Who are you?"

"The Honorable John Goddard." He shook the proffered hand and then resisted the urge to wipe the transferred moistness on his trousers.

"And I'm Mr. Richard Howick," Richard added as he came into the room. "I suspect you'll want to talk to us both."

"Ah, rightly so." The portly gentleman encompassed them all in a glance. "Let's get to it, then, shall we?"

Richard took a seat next to Miranda, close but not touching. John willed his friend to put an arm around her and comfort her. She seemed so small and delicate as if the room and the men within would swallow her whole.

John stood behind an empty chair. He rested a hand on top, reminding himself not to show outward agitation. Once this fool was gone, he and Richard could properly talk with Miranda. "I hardly think it necessary to add law enforcement to what is clearly a private matter." He made sure to add just the right touch of authority to his voice. He wasn't his father's son for nothing. *I won't be cowed by unimportant little men.*

"Ordinarily, I'd agree with you on that count, Mr. Goddard." The constable scratched his chin. "Folks and their domestic problems aren't my concern, unless they've taken to murder." He chuckled, but when no one else joined in, he sobered. "However." He pinned John with a hard stare. "I'm afraid I cannot condone, or even allow, this sort of unwholesome activity to go on. It's corruption of the first order, and will tear this village apart."

"Perhaps you should spell out what exactly you mean." John narrowed his eyes. "The problem with Surrey is everything seems based on rumor and gossip or just plain jealousy and fear of what people don't understand."

"Very well." The lawman scratched a sideburn. "Certain members of the village have indicated Mrs. Craythorne is indulging sexually with you two gentlemen."

"Ah, I see." Anger squeezed John's chest. "You mean to say certain pathetically small dignitaries here in Surrey have decided to make it their mission to see that Miranda's life is made miserable unless the law intervenes. Once her brand of scourge is eradicated then everything will be right as rain?"

"Quite, sir." Constable Barnes puffed out his cheeks. He resembled a bloated squirrel. "There are certain codes of conduct we all need to adhere to. Morality must be upheld. I'm sure you understand."

"Actually, I do not." John pressed his advantage. No one in the village held that sort of power. "What Mrs. Craythorne decides to do in the privacy of her own home is not up for debate."

"Sir, it is if what she's engaging in upsets the natural order around here. I am charged with keeping the peace. If Mrs. Craythorne's actions set the village on its ear, I'm honor bound to do something about it."

"John," Miranda's voice sounded small and defeated, "perhaps we should let the matter drop. It's not worth putting you or Richard at risk."

He wouldn't give up without a proper fight. "It's none of the village's business." John darted a glance to Miranda. She sat composed and pale with her hands clasped so tightly in her lap the knuckles showed white. She didn't look at any of the men. He tried one more tactic. "Mrs. Craythorne's estate is far enough removed from the village proper that no one should be affected by her life or her choices."

The constable nodded. "Oh, I agree, sir. But something must be done since..." He trailed off, his eyes shifting to the left.

"Since?" John forced the question around clenched teeth.

The lawman visibly swallowed. "The estate is owned by Mrs. Craythorne's brother. He's a peer, sir. If this matter were to go to the courts or even the papers, it would have disastrous results for him I would imagine." Constable Barnes let his gaze rest on each of them in turn. "If nothing else, you must look at the bigger issues. You're nice enough gents. Consider that."

A queer hiccupping sob escaped Miranda. She lifted her gaze to John's. "Dear heavens, I never once thought what would happen to Matthew's reputation."

John's heart squeezed to see her so pale and upset. He needed to protect her at all costs. "What happens between a man and a woman isn't the business of the public. I think you can agree on that, Constable."

"Absolutely. And we've already covered that, sir." The lawman rocked on his heels. "In normal circumstances, if a couple was blatantly conducting an affair, thumbing their noses at Society, I'd order the two wed and walk away. The matter could be fixed right and tight."

"That's the rub, isn't it?" Richard leaned back on the settee with an ankle resting on a knee. "And now?" Emotion rasped in his voice.

"Since there are three, it's out of my hands." The constable rubbed his nose. "The local gentry are in agreement, which is why they've gotten me involved." He shifted from foot to foot. "I'm afraid I have to respectfully ask that you three leave Surrey. For the good of the village, you understand."

"What?" Miranda shot to her feet. "This is my home! I cannot simply leave. Where would I go?"

John exclaimed at the same time, "What about the good of Mrs. Craythorne? She's been nothing but kind to this village. This is how that kindness is returned, being cast out of her own home?"

The portly man held up his hands, palm outward. "Believe me, missus, Mr. Goddard, I do understand, but the situation is hardly respectable."

"No, this situation is ridiculous," Richard put in. His face was slowly reddening with suppressed rage.

Constable Barnes shrugged. "Be that as it may, I do need you to go quietly or some of the prominent folks will get the courts involved as I said before. No one wants that."

Richard shook his head. "I'd wager that even now, a concerned citizen is penning a missive to Mrs. Craythorne's brother as we speak—if they haven't done so already."

"It will do them no good." Miranda's soft-spoken insertion didn't affect calm. "My brother had his own wild moments while in Surrey. Why do you think he spends so much time in London? The gossip mongers ran him off too."

Constable Barnes shuddered. "Some of the gentry can be nasty if things don't go their way."

The gentry. John curled a hand into a fist. *That damn Lady Underhill and her need to muck about in other folk's affairs.* He tamped his temper. It wouldn't do to land the constable a facer. For the first time he understood what a coil he'd put Miranda into. "Obviously, removing from Surrey won't happen overnight."

The constable nodded. "You have a month, sir. And there is one more thing."

"Of course there is," Richard murmured. He held John's gaze, clearly looking for permission for a fight.

John shook his head. "Such as?"

"Both you, Mr. Goddard, and Mr. Howick must vacate this property in the interim. If either of you are seen on the premises, you can be detained." Constable Barnes folded his hands over his middle. "The lot of you must leave and never take up residence in Surrey again."

John crushed a fist into his free hand. "What if Richard and I promise never to darken her door? Could Mrs. Craythorne stay in that instance?" At least he could make certain Miranda's life wasn't interrupted. If it meant he'd lose her again, so be it. Her happiness was too important.

"I'm afraid not, Mr. Goddard. My orders are very clear. All three of you must leave Surrey. Together or by yourselves, in thirty days you must be gone."

"What if everything was aboveboard and proper?" No amount of wishing on John's part could make the constable soften.

Constable Barnes scratched a sideburn. "I didn't hear anything about that, Mr. Goddard. I just know what I've been told, but I suppose you could appeal. Though appealing on the grounds of making a threesome proper is a far stretch, I'd have to say."

"That's unfair." Richard stood and his dark eyes flashed fire. "Someone must have planned this in advance."

"I wouldn't know about that, sir. I just do as I'm told. Got my orders from someone higher up than me... well, you understand."

"Unfortunately, I do. Damn politics seeping into the lives of the common folk." Richard's face was a dark thundercloud. He glanced at John. "I'm thinking a certain baroness has too much time on her hands."

"Indeed." John's mind spun with all the implications put forth in this one little meeting. The evening which had held such promise was crumbling around him.

"Right then. Sorry to be the bearer of such foul news. This looked like a ripping good party." The constable tipped the brim of his round hat. "Good night and good luck." He left the room, but his backward glance conveyed a gentle, sad tone.

"I won't leave. I cannot." Miranda shook her head. Her eyes were wide and shadowed with confusion and despair. "What of my birds, my life here, all my plans?"

John glanced at Richard. Imperceptibly, he shook his head. They had to fix this. "Sweeting, don't fret." He edged around the furniture. When he reached her side, he pulled her down onto the settee next to him. "There's an easy solution, and one that will satisfy everyone involved."

"What?" She barely peered at Richard as he sat on her other side.

"Marry me," John urged. He took her hand and threaded their fingers together. "No one can fault you in the eyes of the law then. You'd be wed and thereby take the power from the gossipmongers."

"Capital plan." Richard nodded. He patted her other hand. "I'll fade away, be forgotten overseas. The temptation will be removed."

"No." She twirled an escaped lock of hair around her finger.

"Why?" John felt the tremors in her hand and vowed to help her if he could. "Is it the curse? I must warn you, I'm more powerful than some alleged bad luck, and I don't buy into it by half."

"It's outside of enough that I'm being dictated to on how to live my life." Miranda yanked her hand from John's. "I can't doom you to an early death." She lifted her gaze to his. Moisture spiked her red-gold lashes. "And even if I did agree, what of Richard? I could never hurt him by excluding him, but I can hardly marry both of you, even if I wanted to."

"You let me worry about my own affairs." Richard pressed his lips to the curve of her shoulder. "Our plan is sound, love."

Still, she shook her head and struggled to her feet. "It goes beyond merely the marriage or not portion." Brushing a tear from her cheek, she looked at John. "You both hold important livelihoods that you love. I refuse to jeopardize them for the sake of a relationship we can't indulge in for fear of whispers and rumors."

"Bollocks. Why the hell will you let people like Lady Underhill tell you how to live your life? That's not the woman I know."

"You heard the constable. What else can we do?" Sadness infused her voice, capped off by a waver that nearly had him shedding a tear of his own.

He hated to see her so out of sorts. John launched to his feet. They'd lose her to stubbornness instead of political pressure. "I let you send me away the last time. I won't make the same mistake again." He dropped both hands on her shoulders. The tremor that racked her body transferred to him. "Why are you afraid, Miranda? Surely it goes beyond reputations and avoiding the public eye."

She stroked her fingers along his cheek, her touch feather light, her eyes wide. "I care for you and Richard too much to do anything that will either make you resent me later or destroy your lives." A sob escaped her. She broke from his hold. "Please, John, let me go." She peered at him from beneath her lashes then sliced her gaze to Richard. "You both must forget me. It seems we're no match for the evils of Society, no matter how much we wish it to be otherwise. I'm so sorry."

"Miranda!" John called to her, but she hitched her skirts and ran from the room as if they were both demons from hell.

"That went well." Sarcasm dripped from Richard's voice.

"Shut up." John's shoulders slumped. "Damn it all. Why won't she give in to what she really wants?"

"Perhaps she doesn't realize what she wants." Richard glared. "Let's go track her to earth and show her."

John held up a hand. "Gently. Give her a few minutes to compose herself. Then we'll go." And this time he wasn't letting her out of his sight until she'd consented to be his wife. "This has been one devil of a day."

Chapter Eleven

Miranda wrapped her arms around her middle and let the sobs consume her. The delicate furnishings of her bedroom as well as the dear collectibles and paintings she'd amassed over the years couldn't comfort her—not this time. No matter that she'd tried so hard to avoid scandal and public interest, it had come anyway, and now more reputations would be destroyed than merely hers. John, Richard, Annabelle, her brother and who knew how many others once the tabbies got their claws into whomever would listen. They wouldn't stop until she herself had been brought low and lost everything.

She laid her forehead against the cool window glass and watched the flickering light from a single oil lamp reflect in the pane. Her stomach twisted. Was her reputation more important to her than losing the men who she'd become fond of in such a short period of time? What good was a sterling name if she'd be alone?

A sharp rap on her door scattered her thoughts. She crossed the room, wiping at the moisture on her cheeks as she went. At the door, she said, "So help me, Eppson, if that's you, I'll turn you out this very moment." Her butler's high-handed manipulation still rankled, but how could she terminate his employment after so many years of service simply due to a sixes-and-sevens mood?

The deep chuckle on the other side of the wood didn't belong to her servant. "It's not Eppson. Let me in, Miranda."

"Go away, John. I meant what I said. Leave me alone." Yet flutters brushed her insides. A man interested in only physical relations wouldn't put forth so much effort.

"I'm afraid I cannot do that, but if you persist in being stubborn, I have no issue arguing or declaring myself in the hall. However, I'd rather a private audience." He knocked again. "Let me in."

She gripped the knob, turned it and pulled open the door. Both John and Richard stood in the hall. "Why will the two of you not call 'defeat'?" Though her heart leapt at seeing them, a wave of exhaustion crept over her. A woman simply should never experience such a wide variety of emotions in a short time.

"We English are not in the habit of surrendering." Richard swept into the room. He slid an arm around her waist as he went and pulled her with him, forceful enough that her attempt at escaping was wasted. "And if anyone does, it will be you to us."

"He's quite right. The battle is just beginning, my dear," John added. He closed the door once he'd entered. The unmistakable click of the lock rang in the sudden stillness. "Neither of us will leave without a victory this time. And please don't make this a whole thing about being smothered. Richard and I are merely determined."

Miranda swallowed the remainder of the tears crowding her throat. "What of my guests?" When Richard moved behind her and stroked his palms down her arms, she shivered. "Something must be done with them. They cannot..." Why was it every time one of them touched her she lost the capacity to think clearly?

John joined them. "Your butler has shown them out and discreetly mentioned you'd retired with a headache. Not that they would have stayed anyway, after the whole scene we made down there." He plucked at the onyx-encrusted clasp that held the satin duster closed just beneath her breasts. "In all honestly, Eppson has gotten too cheeky and is in need of a set down."

"He's concerned—"

"No, he's bossy and taking advantage of your good nature. Once you agree to be mine, you will need to turn him out." When John had undone the clasp, Richard slid the duster from her shoulders and down her arms before finally freeing it from her body. The fabric rustled to the floor. "That problem doesn't occur with my servants." John caressed the side of her neck. "Life in my townhouse is much different, but you'll find it runs like clockwork. They'll adapt to your supervision without issue."

She sucked in a ragged breath. "I haven't agreed to anything, let alone moving. Surrey has been my solace, the place where I returned every time my world was turned upside down."

"Now, your life will only do such once more, and you'll remove to London. Sometimes change is good." He winked. "I'm quite certain you'll come around. We're very persuasive, and it's well past time to find a different sort of sanctuary." John's eyes twinkled with secrets she'd give anything to unravel. He turned her about, so she faced Richard. "Tell me—us—why you're afraid. You act as if your soul will split in two over this situation."

Once again, they'd neatly trapped her. While John worked the buttons at the back of her gown, Richard plucked the pins from her hair. Heat licked along her skin from their attention. She knew where it would lead. She darted a glance to the bed then sought out Richard's gaze. His eyes were no less desire-filled than John's. In mere minutes she'd have everything she'd longed for since the men had begun their courtship, yet how could she go through with it when getting close would irrevocably do them harm?

Richard dropped the last pin. He encouraged her tresses to fall about her shoulders. "I believe John is still waiting for your answer." As her dress sagged around her breasts, Richard spun her until she faced John.

"What are you afraid of, sweeting? That you'll become too fond of us or that you already have?" He eased her gown from her bosom then allowed Richard to work it off her arms and down her body.

She gave into the shiver as the cool air wafted over her exposed skin. "I..." Miranda dropped her gaze to focus on John's sapphire stick pin. His eyes were too intense, too full of love and hope—too full of blazing desire. She couldn't bear to see that crumble beneath disappointment, for that's what she'd have to give him. Finally, the tension grew too much. "I'm terrified I'll love you too much and you'll leave me." No matter how badly she wanted to help with the seduction scene they built, she couldn't let herself touch them. Once she did, her reserves would break and she wouldn't stop until she was sated.

Richard pressed a kiss onto her shoulder. The scratch of his mustache sent heightened awareness crashing into her. "We won't leave. We already promised." He worked the buttons at the back of her petticoat and had it off her body in less than a heartbeat. "The three of us cannot be torn apart."

Heat swirled through her. It throbbed between her legs and swelled her breasts. "No, I mean I fear you'll die." Unable to stay away, she crushed John's lapels in her fists. "As soon as we're wed, you'll live on borrowed time. I know. I've seen it three times before, and it won't matter how much I might love you. Feelings won't be able to keep fate from your door. I've tried and failed. I don't have the strength to survive such a thing again."

His eyes lit. "Then you admit you love me." He cupped her face in his big hands while Richard unlaced her stays.

Tingles raced down her spine, as much from the brush of Richard's fingers as John's words. "Perhaps love is too strong a word. And I did say 'might.' I'm fond of you, yes, and of Richard too, but we've known each other for a week only." She shook her head, dislodging John's hands. "This isn't a fairy story. It won't end nice and tidy. We won't ride off on stallions into the sunset. You've seen the evidence of that down in the parlor. There is no happy ending for us."

"Only because you're being stubborn." Richard pulled away the stays. The garment thumped onto the floor. He slid his arms around her waist and pressed close. "A woman in your position has set herself up for a fair shot at a happily ever after. The only thing lacking is the conviction, but we'll shore that up for you."

John nodded. "Two men who are tip-over-tail for you, whose only objectives are to bring you pleasure and protect you from the ugliness of the world, we await your word." He ran the pad of his thumb along her bottom lip. "I don't buy into your curse, Miranda. You'll need a stronger excuse to keep us at bay."

"It's not an excuse. I'm attempting to keep you both safe—alive—and with your reputations intact. Why can you not see that?"

John rolled his eyes. "Why can you not see what we see?"

She fought off the fluttery sensations that wound through her insides as John trailed his fingers down her neck. "I care for you too much to consign you to death. Not to mention such a scandal will jeopardize your careers. It's only a matter of time before word of what we've done spreads out of Surrey."

"I'm not ashamed." Liquid need slid through her insides at John's smile. "Richard and I can worry about our vocations. If anything is said, it will be treated as rumors or gossip. Outside of Surrey, the rest of the world hasn't a concern toward the three of us. To all outward purposes, I'll be married to you and that's all anyone needs to know."

"But..." Why wouldn't he understand the greater problem, and she'd never told him yes?

"Love, we all will die eventually." Richard smoothed his palms over her hips. Then, inch by slow inch, he drew up the hem of her shift. "Why not derive the most pleasure we can from life while we're able?"

She licked her lips. "Any relationship needs balance. How can ours be such when there are three? Someone's bound to be left out from physical pleasure, emotional stability or anything else."

"That won't happen with us." John cupped her breasts. He rubbed his thumbs over her hardening nipples through the fabric.

Miranda stifled a moan. She couldn't give into them yet. There was too much at stake. "How can you be so certain?"

"Richard will be in the field much of the time. When he comes home, your attention naturally will belong to him and to us both when the need for the *ménage* comes to the forefront, and no, I'm not concerned. Overbearing country dragons do not hold my interest."

She wanted to cry with frustration, but the men's overwhelming caresses nearly had her undone. "Yes, and in the meanwhile, both you and John will be free to live to your heart's content, carefree men without a care. I'll bear the brunt of the stigma, the bulk of the talk, the weight of the whispers behind fans."

"This is true." Richard nipped her neck. "Chances are they won't stop vilifying your character because you'll command the attentions of an eligible bachelor—me—even though you'll be married to John." As the shift bunched at her waist, Richard slid a hand between her thighs. "But I'll defend you until my dying day. Gossips have no bearing on what I want."

"They'll still talk then. How do I combat that?"

"You don't. It's just gossip, sweetness. Don't mind them," Richard whispered. "You may be the scandal of the moment, but in the nature of all scandals, there will be another one to come along soon that will make people forget yours." He moved his fingers over her folds. "You can enjoy your domestic life under the guise of respectability and once I return to

England's shores, John and I will give you the fuck together that you've dreamed of."

Miranda sighed from the decadence. Need streaked through her core the second Richard rubbed a finger over her nub. She sighed. Familiar pleasure shivered along her limbs, and the fire that had started earlier in the study erupted into an inferno, even more so when John rolled her distended nipples. *I have to focus. Tumbling into bed won't solve the problem.* The most pressing issue surged to the forefront of her mind. "How can I leave Surrey, my manor house? Everything I love is here." She dropped her head back to rest on Richard's shoulder. *Why do they have to be so distracting?*

"Except us." Richard's breath steamed her ear. "We're not here, nor can we be due to our livelihoods. You know this. Why rely on such a feeble excuse?"

John bent his head to suck at a nipple through the thin lawn of her shift. Miranda arched her back, pushing her breast farther into his mouth. Richard strummed his fingers along her folds then returned to tormenting her swollen nubbin. When John lifted his head, his eyes gleamed like sapphires. "You already know London is our destination. Would you throw everything away for a mere pile of bricks and some acreage dotted with bird droppings? Memories make a home. You can carry them anywhere, and you don't even own this property. Your brother can swoop in and reclaim it from you at his whim. What then?"

Put in such a light, Miranda had no choice but to acknowledge his side of the argument. If she remained in Surrey, she'd be alone with neither man to warm her arms or fill her life. In London, she'd spend the time with both, at least while Richard was home. But how could she leave her birds? Damn the impossible men. Was it true she wanted them more than mere material objects? She held John's gaze and fought back a smile at the knowing twinkle in his eyes. Besides, she'd have John all to herself in Richard's absence, which was what she'd wanted ever since that long ago house party, the first time she'd fallen for him. "I suppose I wouldn't throw it all away for that."

A low sound of triumph rang in her ear followed by a nip to her lobe by Richard. "I'm so glad you're coming around to our way of thinking."

She fought off a smile, not wanting to give either of them the satisfaction of winning her over so quickly. "It's not fair. There are two of you and only one of me. This discussion is already stilted and won't go in my favor."

"This is true." Richard's movements against her button grew more frantic. "But then, I would think any woman who finds herself in the company of two men bent on nothing more than her pleasure would be in very favorable straits indeed."

Miranda sighed. Need circled through her belly and bore down in ever-increasing bands the longer Richard played. He plucked her bud at the same time John teased a nipple with his teeth. "Oh, oh..." Already primed, her body stiffened as the sweet pressure broke and crested into gentle release. Her inner muscles pulsed, drawing out the pleasure, and she melted against John's chest. "That was lovely."

John's laughter rumbled beneath her ear long before it broke from his throat. "I grow tired of hearing you say our carnal play is just 'lovely,' darling. We shall need to rectify this."

"Will I finally see you both naked? It's been dreadfully unfair to deprive me of this the whole time the scandal has played out. If I'm to be terrorized by petty gentry, I should at least get a treat." She didn't protest when John tugged the shift over her head and off her body. She stood before them in her jeweled choker as well as her stockings, garters, and shoes. While she didn't mind being vulnerable, the fact they still wore their evening attire caused her to snort with annoyance. "Gentlemen?"

Both of them raked her body with their gazes, leaving her trembling with hot longing as if they'd touched her. Her heartbeat thundered through her veins. Her breath caught. Finally, after what seemed like endless seconds, John crushed her into his arms and kissed her as if she alone held the world's air and he wanted it all. The warmth of his hands at her ribs branded her; the scrape of his evening coat on her sensitized nipples wrenched a gasp from her mouth. Richard pulled her from John's grasp and kissed her with the force and intensity she'd come to expect from him. He nipped at her lips, even lightly bit the bottom one—claiming her. He bossed her tongue with his, threaded his fingers into her hair and plundered her mouth, searching out the interior as if hunting for secrets.

Miranda broke the kiss for nothing more than to have a chance to breathe. She glanced from one man to the other. "Either take me to bed or leave. I'll drown beneath your onslaught."

"Capital idea, don't you think, Richard?" John's chuckle sent goose flesh sailing over her skin. "Why don't I divest Mrs.

Craythorne of her stockings while you undress? It won't do to keep such a needy woman waiting. Poor thing."

Moisture trickled between her thighs, but she had no time to marvel that John's words did such things to her for he knelt then slid his hands down her left leg to her foot. The rasp of Richard's clothes as he shed them filled the thick silence. She couldn't spare him a thought, couldn't even look his way as John occupied her full attention. Gently lifting her foot, he removed her shoe and tossed it aside. After pressing a kiss to her knee, he untied her garter. With agonizing slowness, he rolled down the silk then again lifted her foot and tugged the hosiery from her limb. He placed her foot back down then ran his hands up the length of her leg. After his long fingers brushed her damp curls, he switched attention to her other leg and began the sensual process all over again.

"You wouldn't be so cruel as to draw out the torture, would you?" Miranda dug her fingers into his shoulders while he eased his fingertips over her skin. Up and down the outsides of her legs. Swirling patterns along the ticklish backs of her knees. When he pressed baby kisses to her curls, she moaned, and her knees wobbled.

"Absolutely, but first, I'll let Richard drive you insane while I undress."

And then Richard was there, petting and soothing his hands over her skin. His engorged cock brushed her curls. "You've been hiding a goddess' body beneath your clothes."

"How you do go on." But pleasure rode her spine all the same. For the first time she didn't mind the extra weight she'd put on with each marriage. Her indulgent men made her feel like the most cherished woman in the world.

"It's nothing except the truth." He slid his palms down her sides, counted each rib before glancing over her hips. "I adore your curves." The naughty man kissed her while at the same time grasping her naked rear end. He squeezed her buttocks and pulled her tight against his erection. "I can't wait to pound into your heat." He nuzzled her neck above the choker. "I want to hear you moan my name."

Miranda shivered as the tip of his cock teased her hidden nub. Nearby, John's soft curses filled the silence. From the sound of his hopping, he'd gotten a foot caught in his trousers. She stifled a laugh. *Serves him right.*

She edged away from Richard in order to run her palms over his contoured chest. A sprinkling of light brown hair covered the clear skin. She spent endless seconds tracing his flat abdomen and urging her fingertips along the defined muscles there. "It should be a crime to look as you do." Now that he wasn't tormenting her, clarity returned to an extent. "But, it's my turn to explore and make you ache for me." Without further preamble, she dropped to her knees before him. His hard member bobbed near her face. Gently, she cupped his sac, giving it a squeeze. When he choked back a gasp, she grinned. "Let's see what you taste like, shall we?"

"God, Miranda, no—" A gurgling moan took away Richard's protest as she licked his shaft from root to tip.

A giggle escaped her. "If you think I'd let your oral teasing of me go unnoticed, you don't know me that well." She repeated the action and savored the salty, earthy taste of him. "Poor Richard." She kissed his cock head and then swirled her tongue around it. "Whatever would the Home Office say if they found out you were defeated by having your cock sucked? Imagine if the French knew this little secret."

Close behind her, John laughed. "Make him go weak, Miranda. Teach him a lesson. He's entirely too full of himself."

Richard's laugh blended with John's. "Soon, she'll be full of us."

Her nipples tightened. She slid a hand to a breast and pinched a distended nub. Sensation streaked through her breasts to lodge between her thighs. Both men groaned. Oh, how she wished they'd take her to bed. *Silly men, still needing to play the game.*

She lifted her gaze to John's. "Mind your manners, John. I intend to do the same to you." Feeling quite smug at his look of anticipation, she gave Richard her full attention. Miranda slid her hands around to his buttocks. Firm and muscled as the rest of him, they clenched at her touch. She grinned, opened her mouth and took his rigid cock inside, sliding along his length until she hit his balls. Afterward, she retreated just as slowly. She sucked on the sensitive tip then released long enough to swirl her tongue and find the veins that decorated the soft skin. Richard's cock pulsed and thickened. When he slid his hands into her hair and thrust into her mouth, she moved with him, sucking at the tip every time he pulled back.

"Best not make him spend before we tumble you into bed. There will be time enough for such things." John eased her from Richard. His member glistened. "My turn."

"My pleasure." And it was. Though she wildly loved sex, with all her husbands, she'd let them make love to her mouth but she hadn't enjoyed it, treating it like a chore to endure. With Richard and John, it was something she wanted to do in order to please them as well as herself. After so much teasing, it was only natural. She moved slightly and knelt before John. From her vantage point, he seemed even taller and more massive. Unlike Richard, a mat of dark hair spread across his chest with a ribbon tapering over his flat abdomen and ending in a wealth of dark curls framing an impressive erection.

He fisted his cock and tapped the end against her lips. “Like what you see?”

“I always have.” Where Richard’s member was thicker, John’s was longer and thinner. Miranda swirled her tongue around its swollen head and licked a drop of moisture that had seeped from the slit. Tangy and salty, his taste lingered on her palate. She hooked one hand at his thigh then guided him into her mouth. He hit the back of her throat all too soon without her taking in all of him. Undeterred, she wrapped her free hand around his base, squeezing and twisting while she bobbed on his length.

“It would seem our lover is quite skilled in the bedroom arts.” Richard knelt behind her and cupped her breasts. “I wonder what else she can do.”

She moaned around John’s cock. Desire pulsed through her passage. *I need both men, and soon.*

“Dear God, I never thought...” John gripped the back of her head, keeping her still as he thrust with an even rhythm. “You’re so warm.” His cock jumped. On one of her more enthusiastic suckles, he yanked from her mouth so abruptly her teeth scraped his skin. “Blast it. I won’t last if we continue.”

Miranda licked her lips and then pouted. “Neither of you will let me taste you as you spend?”

"Most definitely; however, now is not that time." John extended a hand, and when she slipped her fingers into his palm, he brought her to her feet. "I've waited too long to claim you as properly as I've wanted."

"You did claim me, in the stillroom, remember?"

"That wasn't proper."

A shudder racked her body at the desire in his expression—the same thing she felt for him. She stood on tiptoe, cupped his face, and brought his lips to hers. When she pulled back, emotions twinkled in his eyes, emotions she desperately wanted to believe in and explore. "Come to bed, John." Turning, she stepped into Richard's waiting embrace and kissed him in the same manner. She smiled. "Come to bed, Richard. I want my men to send me flying."

The tendons in Richard's neck worked with his heavy swallow. "As if we could deny you anything." He climbed onto the bed and reclined on his back against the pillows. His aroused cock pointed to the ceiling, a bead of moisture gleaming on its head. "Ride me, Miranda." Strain grated through his command.

"Truly?" Her heartbeat accelerated. She'd assumed command of a coupling only twice before in her lifetime. The opportunity to do so now had her stomach fluttering.

"Yes, come. And in a timely manner."

John gave her bottom a swat as she joined Richard on the bed. "He doesn't relinquish power all that often. Seize the day."

When she straddled Richard, his rigid length rubbed her rear. The mattress dipped as John joined them. The touch of his hand on her back both calmed and unnerved her. She'd dreamed about having them both in her bed, and now that the moment had arrived, doubts stole in. Briefly, she glanced at John. "Will you take me at the same time?" Of course she'd heard stories whispered in passing while at the market or attending the opera in London of sexual exploits, but she was never sure how such things happened in real life.

"No, love." John pressed a line of tender kisses along her spine. "At least not tonight. It's been challenging enough on its own already. You're not ready, and I'd rather not force such a thing upon you without discussing it first or preparing you."

"Oh." A mix of relief and disappointment washed over her.

Richard grasped one of her hands. "But that doesn't mean we both won't love you fiercely now." He moved his hips, and his hard length brushed her buttocks. "Unless you'd like me to spend all over your coverlet, I suggest you get on with it."

Smiling, Miranda stared at him. "Don't be a bloody bully." She rose up on her knees, took his cock in hand then slammed down on him, impaling herself fully. A wealth of sensation sped through every particle of her being. Her breasts tingled. Her channel pulsed around his member as she adjusted and let him fill her. "Dear heavens this is wonderful."

"Damnation, Miranda, if you don't start..." The threat, said between clenched teeth died off when she did, in fact, begin to move.

The novelty of finding herself in the position of power during intercourse captivated her. She leaned forward, and that slight change caused her button to rub against the base of his member. Shivery feeling ebbed through her passage, and she moaned. John's hands on her back forced her down even farther. Her aroused nipples scraped Richard's chest. Tingling sensation had her at the edge. She sat upright and rotated her hips. The way he felt inside her, leaving no part untouched, made her head spin and the terrible pressure in her core built once again.

Richard grasped her waist, guiding her, moving her along his length as he thrust upward. "Meet me, love. Work against me for the best advantage and take what you want."

She nodded. Every time he shoved, she plunged downward. Soon, they struck a rhythm, and the slap of wet flesh filled the room. John took position behind her. His cock poked into the small of her back, hot and hard. He reached around to finger her nubbin over and over, perfectly matching the rhythm she and Richard had found. Miranda gasped. Was this what happened during a *ménage* then? Both men working in tandem to make their woman shatter? Her arousal spiked, circling through her body like a hungry serpent. She continued to bounce, impaling herself again and again on Richard's member. Spirals of need danced up her spine. Pinpricks of pain and delight raced through her as John rolled her nipples and worked her button. Her breathing shallowed. Sweat dampened her neck beneath her hair. Being with Richard resembled riding a runaway carriage on a slippery hill in the dark. The fluttering in her stomach was exactly the same since she'd experienced just that years ago. It was both thrilling and a tiny bit scary. She rocked her body on top of his, sawing his length, barely tipping off before taking him back inside her wet passage.

Richard dug his fingers into her hips. "Quickly." His upward thrusts grew more erratic and forceful enough that she saw starbursts behind her closed eyes.

Then John's fingers renewed their questing at her nubbin and the dam inside her broke. "Richard!" Waves of pleasure crashed over her and washed her away on an intense tide of bliss. Her body sagged backward, held upright by John's arms around her. She rested her head on his shoulder. While her inner walls squeezed Richard's member, he thrust again and then his seed shot free to warm her passage.

As his cock pulsed in time to her contractions, John eased her over Richard's chest with gentle hands. Richard wrapped his arms around her. He pressed a kiss to her forehead. "I knew I wouldn't be disappointed with you, Mrs. Craythorne."

She nuzzled the crook of his neck, tasting sweat on her tongue. Her heart trembled in perfect time to her ragged heartbeat. With Richard, she felt feminine and every bit a still-desirable woman even at her advanced age according to society. She opened her eyes to see his dear face. "I can tell you this: I will always look forward to welcoming you back to England." The thought of joining with him after months of separation, consumed by frantic need and white-hot desire, sent shivers through her core. "Please be certain you come home to me."

Chapter Twelve

No sooner had Miranda elected to snuggle against Richard's sweat-slicked body than John lay beside him and situated her between them on her back.

"I hope you're not too tired, sweeting. I haven't had my turn yet." The low rumble of his voice, coupled with his desire-darkened eyes, loosed goose flesh over her skin. Her nipples pebbled while new need burgeoned through her core. Miranda marveled that she craved another go after what Richard had just given her. John partially covered her body with his while Richard rolled to one side. "Let me show you how much I want you."

She twined her hands around his neck and wriggled into a more comfortable position beneath him. The feel of his large, muscled frame against her softer curves made her feel protected and cherished all at once. Her stomach clenched. It was all she'd ever wanted from life; why she'd married three times before. John magnified everything, multiplied it a hundred-fold and gave it back to her. *I'd be an idiot not to agree to his suit.* But the moment at hand and her building need scattered her deeper thoughts. "You won't allow me to ride you?"

"No. I'm not as lazy as my friend over there." John spread her thighs with a knee and settled between the cradle of her bent legs. The coarse hair on his chest caused frenzied frissons of excitement to dance over her skin.

Richard snorted. "Give me an hour or so and I'll show you who's lazy." While kneeling to one side, he brushed the hair from her forehead and smiled into her face. "John's not as intense, but the ladies seem to enjoy him. The bugger's got impressive length."

Chills climbed her spine, and not from being moments away from feeling John inside her again. "I should hope that from this point forward, the two of you realize you belong exclusively to me." She glanced between them. "If you expect me to be loyal to you, I want the same respect." Her chest squeezed. Her chin quivered. "I refuse to give you my heart only for you to trample on it if someone better, prettier or wealthier turns your head."

"Dearest, how can you even think that?" John brushed his lips against hers. He lowered his big body. "It's been you who I've chased for a while now. Only you." He rested the bulk of his weight on his forearms. "Marry me. In all the years since I saw you at that house party, I've never strayed from the dream of making you mine."

"Oh John." She stroked her fingers along the side of his face. Her passion ramped as his stubble scratched her palm. "London is so dirty part of the year, and noisy and crowded the rest of the time. Besides, what will I do with my birds?" It was a weak argument at this stage, but she wanted to give one last bid for independence before settling into John's well-ordered life.

He nipped a line of playful kisses beneath her jaw. "I own a townhouse on Chesterfield Street in Mayfair. It has a small garden in the back." He nibbled on her earlobe. "I'll allow you to bring two peacocks though the rest will need to stay here and get on without you. Let your brother worry about them."

"Poultry aside, you two can thumb your noses at Society while cavorting right under their noses." Richard trailed a hand down the side of her neck. "And when I'm home you can welcome me with open arms…" He kissed her with enough heat she feared she'd dissolve into the bed clothes. When he lifted his head, his eyes sparkled. "…and wide-open legs."

A hard pulse stole through her core. She shivered. "Dear heavens."

"Always without tact, Richard." John's voice rumbled in her ear. His breath steamed her cheek. "Don't mind him."

Tendrils of desire sailed through her insides. A sigh escaped. She almost surrendered to his touch before recalling herself back to the moment. "What of the budgies and the cockatoo?" *I cannot imagine not having their cheery little faces greeting me every day.*

John lifted his head in order to hold her gaze. "Bring four budgies. Put them in a smaller cage that will comfortably occupy a corner of the damn parlor. You can haul the cockatoo up to London as well, but please, for the love of God, say you'll marry me. Put both of us out of our misery, woman."

She turned her head and assessed Richard. Strain and worry, deepened by the flickering oil lamp, showed in his expression. Tingles rushed through her core at the thought of coupling with him again and for as long as she wished it. Then her thoughts moved into the dark place of imagining both men in her body simultaneously. She could almost feel the movement of both of their cocks inside her, but the exact logistics of how it would work escaped her. *I will need to ask them for that very thing, and soon, lest I go mad from wondering.* "But..." She also wanted to be a source of stability in his otherwise helter-skelter existence and to give him hope that someone cared when he was away. Then she peered into John's face. Concern mixed with unbreakable love in his eyes. Her heart skipped. He'd been at the back of her mind and firmly rooted in her thoughts even if she hadn't been fully aware of him. His devotion had always been true, and she realized now she'd come to depend on him.

Miranda sighed. "I'll miss Surrey. It pains me we can never return here."

"I promise to badger my father into letting us use his home in the north if you wish to commune with nature or enjoy a brief reprieve from London."

"If Surrey's society turns me out, what makes you think your father's village will accept me?"

"Because, my darling, you'll be mine, and to us Goddards, family means more than idle gossip. My father had a wild enough past, besides. He'll understand."

"Oh." He'd truly thought of everything. "That might be acceptable."

"Then you'll take my name and embrace the *ménage* relationship?" John dropped a kiss to the corner of her mouth—teasing, tempting, pleading.

"Yes, only if you understand the risk you both take by winning me."

John's low laughter reverberated deep in her chest. "I don't fear fate because I love you more."

She lost another piece of her heart to him. "Charmer." She stroked a hand down his back and sighed at the play of muscles beneath her fingers. "It's a wonder you and I didn't cause a scandal years ago."

That brought out a laugh from Richard. "Believe me, love, he wanted to, but he was too much of a gentleman to throw over Oliver or even your third husband. He's loyal to a fault." He tugged on a lock of her hair. "I don't fear fate either. I'd fight a thousand of Napoleon's men for the chance to be with you."

She slipped her free hand around Richard's neck and brought him in for a kiss. "Thank you." How did she think she could resist them?

John continued, "And you'll be happy if we happen to start a family, even though you might not know which one of us fathered any children we may have?"

Flutters darted through her stomach. *Children. A family.* Tears prickled the backs of her eyelids. "I will, except in all my years of marriage, fortune has never blessed me with children. It would seem I'm truly living under a cloud of bad luck."

"No, you've merely never met the man—men—who wanted you badly enough that you might allow yourself to dream of the possibilities." John claimed her lips in a kiss so tender she cried. He teased her with butterfly brushes then drew his tongue along the seam of her mouth until she opened and invited him in. Heated satin tangled with slick silk as they dueled together. When he broke the kiss, he was as breathless as she. The insistent weight of his hard cock rested on her thigh. "Your answer, madam."

"Yes," Richard added. "Please don't keep us in suspense."

She smiled. Her John was determined, she'd give him that. No wonder he'd been an excellent Runner. And Richard, she could just imagine him bedeviling various foreign dignitaries and ambassadors. "Yes, I'll marry you." When John would have embraced her, she stopped him with her palms against his chest. "However, I warn you. I don't intend to quit being the woman I am simply for matrimony. I've learned my lessons well in the past."

"But—"

She pressed her fingers to his lips to silence him. "I want my freedom too. If I choose to match make in London, so be it. If I choose to enter a different profession, you must allow me the space to find my calling."

"Mmmhmm." He nodded then nipped at her fingers.

"I dislike a man attempting to control where I go and what I do simply because he's wed to me." She glanced at Richard. "Or bedding me." Her gaze slid back to John. "No matter how fond I am of you or how much I'll love you more as time goes on, you must trust me. I can be my own person while belonging to you." Miranda held his gaze, almost drowning in the blue depths. "Understand?" She drew her hand beneath his chin then downward to stroke the strong column of his neck.

"Yes." Again, he nodded. "I promise. You can pursue whatever dream your heart desires for I've already met mine." He grasped her hands, twined her fingers with his then drew them over her head and pinned them to the pillows. Her nipples scraped against his hairy chest, renewing her need. Liquid heat pooled between her thighs.

For the first time since John and Richard began their unorthodox courtship, Miranda allowed herself to look forward to the future. She swallowed the unshed tears crowding her throat and turned her head to capture Richard's gaze. "If you even think of straying, you can leave right this second. I won't waste a thought on you while you're in the field if you hope to charm some perfumed, French light-skirt."

"I know better than that, love." He pressed his lips to hers in a kiss that was surprisingly gentle for Richard. "I'm not addle-pated enough to stray when I know I have a prime article waiting for me."

She couldn't contain her grin. "With you two, I never had a chance, did I?"

"No, you bloody well did not." Richard stroked the side of her face then followed the line of her neck and swept along the curve of one breast to tweak a nipple. He laughed when she bit back a moan.

John chuckled. "Now, will there be much more talking? I'd like to make love to the soon-to-be Mrs. Goddard. I deserve a damned commendation for postponing release this long."

"No more talking." Miranda tugged at his hands, but he didn't release her. Switching tactics, she wriggled her hips. Tingles swept through her core when his length rubbed against her swollen nub. "I need you inside me."

He wasted no time. With one smooth stroke, he pushed inside her passage, inch by inch, until he was fully sheathed. His groan blended with hers. "I swear I'll never become accustomed to how good you feel." John withdrew and the tip of his cock flirted with her entrance.

Miranda squeezed his fingers. She was already lost to the wonder of him. Tilting her hips, she met his shallow thrusts. Each penetration sent shivery sensation through her core. Each brush played havoc with her inner walls, but fell short of hitting that special spot. "John..."

"I know what you need." John released her hands and pulled out. When she whimpered a protest, he tsked under his breath. "Patience." He knelt, grasped her legs in his big hands and eased her knees around his waist. "Hold steady there, love. The best is yet to come."

She did as he instructed. "Just..." Her words died in her throat as he shoved into her slick passage with full force, not stopping until every bit of him filled her. Miranda tightly closed her eyes in an effort to savor his feel and the tightness and the flutters that raced through her channel each time he did little except breathe.

A tremor racked her body the second Richard took a nipple into his mouth. His mustache tickled her skin. He rolled the other, plucking it in time to John's thrusts. Miranda moaned. *Dear heavens, dual pleasuring is wonderful.* It was so much more than one man could deliver on his own, so much bigger and all-consuming. *I rather like this turn of events.* The intense onslaught overwhelmed her, threatened to sink her beneath its tide. Waves of need stacked tight in her core, pushing downward, but she fought against imminent release. She wasn't ready to end the exquisite torment yet.

Then John changed his pace. Instead of the slow, loving strokes, his thrusts became longer and faster with greater force behind them. Every time he pushed, her body slid along the bed. She opened her eyes and stretched her hands, planting them against the headboard, and still John's hips worked.

Richard released her nipple with a slight *pop*. He squeezed and massaged her breasts before returning to rub his fingers over the sensitive tips. Shivers raced from her breasts to her core, colliding with the excitement already filling her insides.

"Oh, I'm so close." Her whisper didn't seem to have an effect on either man for they continued their joint assault. She could do nothing except enjoy it.

The raw slap of John's stones against her wet flesh filled the silence, punctuated with his slight moans and Richard's murmured words of encouragement. Miranda thrashed her head from side to side. She'd tear apart soon, and it wouldn't be a matter of flying anymore. She'd explode from need. Her thighs quivered with strain. Her breasts and nipples burned from Richard's play. Her passage vibrated with warning contractions. Richard crept a hand down her body and strummed her button. The pulses increased to full-fledged tremors. "More. Harder. Please." Hot desire threatened to choke her. She bucked against Richard's fingers and John's questing cock.

In the end, her body wasn't as strong as her willpower. When Richard pinched her swollen nub, she shattered. Blissful heat flooded her body and she lost control. As pleasure filled every part of her body, she cried out. John pushed inside once more. His member twitched and jumped. Then the warm stream of his seed raced into her convulsing passage as he followed her with his own release. Richard circled her nub a couple of times, which sent her softly over the edge once more.

He pulled away from her sex. After pressing a gentle kiss to her mouth, he stretched out beside her, his body warm against hers.

John slumped on top of her with her name on his lips.

Miranda relaxed her legs and held him close. She stroked her hands over his sweat-slicked back. His thundering heartbeat matched hers; his ragged breathing echoed in her ear. She turned her head and brushed her lips against the side of his neck. "John, that was—"

"If you say lovely I'll turn you over my knee and spank you." He lifted slightly off and looked into her face.

Desire throbbed between her thighs. Now that would be interesting, but she giggled. "No, it was wonderful. I loved having you inside me and Richard's hands on me. I think we'll all get on quite well." She threaded the fingers of one hand through the thick hair at John's neck while she grabbed one of Richard's with the other. "I'm looking forward to starting our life together." She kissed John then leaned over and did the same to Richard. "I'm glad you didn't give up on me all together."

"Never, love." Richard squeezed her hand.

"Not while I still have breath." John brushed a strand of hair from her forehead. "Shall we rest here for a while before Richard and I send you through your paces again? There is much we can introduce you to."

She heaved a shuddering sigh but nodded. Her heart felt near to bursting with joy. The future had never held so many possibilities, and not one of them included being the victim of misfortune.

Maybe there did need to be a balance between personal satisfaction and scandal in one's life. After all, if scandal hadn't literally come calling, she'd never have reconciled with John or met Richard, and both men were too dear to be forgotten in a morass of morals or cowering from fear of bad luck—whether from her own making or someone else's interference. She made her own fate, and she couldn't wait to see what happened.

The End

Find the continuing adventures of Miranda, Richard, and John in...

Staircase Encounter

Miranda Ellis Mason Craythorne Goddard finally married the one who got away. Though she's secured the amorous interest of two handsome gentlemen, and it's a feat not many women can claim, the third in her trio has been abroad for months.

Mr. John Goddard still can't believe his good fortune. When Miranda consented to be his wife and make a respectable front with him in London, he'd become the happiest of men. He wants nothing more than to set up a nursery, yet the absence of his good friend has taken a bit of the excitement out of the romps.

Richard Howick, a spy who is rarely on English soil, shows up at John's London townhouse unexpectedly and with an appetite for erotic entertainment. After all, he well and truly won the fair widow the same as his friend. When he catches Miranda unaware and carnal pleasure ensues, the fires burn as hot as ever.

That encounter on the staircase will change all of their lives forever in ways neither man could ever imagine.

Warning: at 5K words, this is a short story. For longer novels, please browse the Scandal in Surrey collection.

Regency-era romances by Sandra Sookoo

Colors of Scandal series

Dressed in White
Draped in Green
Trimmed in Blue
Wrapped in Red
Graced in Scarlet
Adorned in Violet
Embellished in Mauve
Clad in Midnight
Garbed in Purple
Resplendent in Ruby
Cloaked in Shadows
Decorated in Christmas
Tangled in Lavender
Persuasive in Pink
Disguised in Tartan (coming April 2022)
Attired in Highland Gold (coming April 2022)
Hopeful in Yellow (coming August 2022)
Imperfect in Peridot (coming October 2022)
Christmas in Crimson (coming November 2022)

Storme Brothers series

The Soul of a Storme
The Heart of a Storme
The Look of a Storme
A Storme's Christmas Legacy
A Storme's First Noelle (in the *Star of Light* anthology)
The Sting of a Storme
The Touch of a Storme
The Fury of a Storme (coming May 2022)

Home for the Holidays series

The Folly of Caroling

Three Mistletoe Kisses
Silver Bells Scandal
A Holly and Ivy Affair

Lords of the Night series

Devil Take the Duke
Bitten by the Earl
Adrift with the Viscount
Treasured by the Earl
Transformed by a Christmas Star
Pistols at Dawn, Your Grace, as part of the *Shifting Hearts* boxed set

Willful Winterbournes series

Romancing Miss Quill (coming June 2022)
Pursuing Mr. Mattingly (coming August 2022)
Courting Lady Yeardly (coming October 2022)
Teasing Miss Atherby (coming late 2022 or early 2023?)

Singular Sensation series

One Little Indiscretion (coming July 2022)
One Secret Wish (coming September 2022)
One Tiny On-Dit Later (coming January 2023)
One Accidental Night with an Improper Duke (coming March 2023)
One Scandalous Choice (coming May 2023)
One Thing Led to Another (coming July 2023)
One Too Many Suitors (coming September 2023)
One Thing Led to Another (November 2023)

Mary and Bright series

A Mary and Bright Christmastide (coming December 2023)
A Springtime Engagement (TBA)
An Autumnal Partnership (TBA)

Diamonds of London series

My Dear Mr. Ridley (coming February 14, 2023)
The Clever Widow's Wager (coming April 23, 2023)
Catch Her if You Can (coming June 13, 2023)
Yours Respectfully, My Lord (coming August 15, 2023)
When the Duke Said Yes (coming September 14, 2023)
To Love a Ghostly Lord (coming October 17, 2023)
One Hell of a Christmas (coming November 20, 2023)

Along Came Tess (coming January 16, 2024)
The Duke's Valentine (coming February 13, 2024
Not in His Usual Style (coming March 12, 2024)
The Merry Month of May (coming April 16, 2024)
The Duchess Problem (coming May 14, 2024)
Spirited Away by the Viscount (June 11, 2024)

Thieves of the Ton series
Captivated by an Adventurous Lady
Engaged to a Scandalous Earl
Married on a Wicked Morning
Intrigued by an Ancient Pedigree
Beguiled on a Christmas Morning: Christmas novella
Caught with a Stolen Diamond
Tortured by a Horrible Secret
Delighted on a Summer's Evening
Trapped in the British Museum
Charmed at a Yuletide Ball
One Silent Night
Redeeming a Tarnished Lord
Lords of Happenstance series
What the Stubborn Viscount Desires
What a Wayward Lord Needs
What the Dashing Duke Deserves
Scandal in Surrey series
Lady Parker's Grand Affair
The Bride's Gambit
Misfortune's Lady
Miss Bennett's Naughty Secret
Standalone Regency romances
Lady Isabella's Splendid Folly
Wagering on Christmas
Magic in Mayflowers
Act of Pardon

Angel's Master
Storm Tossed Rogue
Claiming His Wife
Scoundrel's Trespass
On a Midnight Clear
A Fowl Christmastide
His Pretend Duchess
Visions of Christmastide
An Accidental Countess
A Rogue for Lady Peacock (coming September 2022)
The Most Wonderful Earl of the Year (coming November 2022)
Snowflakes for the Earl (coming December 2022)
She's Got a Duke to Keep Her Warm (coming December 2022)
The Most Wonderful Earl of the Year (coming December 2022)
The Lyon's Dilemma (Lyon's Den connected world) (coming January 2023)

Author Bio

Sandra Sookoo is a *USA Today* bestselling author who firmly believes every person deserves acceptance and a happy ending. Most days you can find her creating scandal and mischief in the Regency-era, serendipity and happenstance in Victorian America or snarky, sweet humor in the contemporary world. Most recently she's moved into infusing her books with mystery and intrigue. Reading is a lot like eating fine chocolates—you can't just have one. Good thing books don't have calories!

When she's not wearing out computer keyboards, Sandra spends time with her real-life Prince Charming in central Indiana where she's been known to goof off and make moments count because the key to life is laughter. A Disney fan since the age of ten, when her soul gets bogged down and her imagination flags, a trip to Walt Disney World is in order. Nothing fuels her dreams more than the land of eternal happy endings, hope and love stories.

Stay in Touch

Sign up for Sandra's bi-monthly newsletter and you'll be given exclusive excerpts, cover reveals before the general public as well as opportunities to enter contests you won't find anywhere else.

Just send an email to sandrasookoo@yahoo.com with SUBSCRIBE in the subject line.

Or follow/friend her on social media:

Facebook: https://www.facebook.com/sandra.sookoo

Facebook Author Page: https://www.facebook.com/sandrasookooauthor/

Pinterest: https://www.pinterest.com/sandrasookoo/

Instagram: https://www.instagram.com/sandrasookoo/

BookBub Page: https://www.bookbub.com/authors/sandra-sookoo

Don't miss out!

Visit the website below and you can sign up to receive emails whenever Sandra Sookoo publishes a new book. There's no charge and no obligation.

https://books2read.com/r/B-A-PDBB-QRLE

BOOKS 2 READ

Connecting independent readers to independent writers.

www.ingramcontent.com/pod-product-compliance
Ingram Content Group UK Ltd.
Pitfield, Milton Keynes, MK11 3LW, UK
UKHW040006200726
13854UKWH00001B/58